I0777754

NIGHT GAMES

A NOVEL

JOSH POWELL & JOEY POWELL

MADAXEMEDIA.COM

PART I: PEOPLE OF THE RED NIGHT
BY JOSH POWELL

PART II: GO TO HELL
BY JOEY POWELL

Published by Mad Axe Media

Edited by Nico Bell

Cover Illustration by Raven Moth Studios

Cover & Interior Design by Joey Powell

Print ISBN: 978-1-966497-06-6

E-Book ISBN: 978-1-966497-07-3

PART

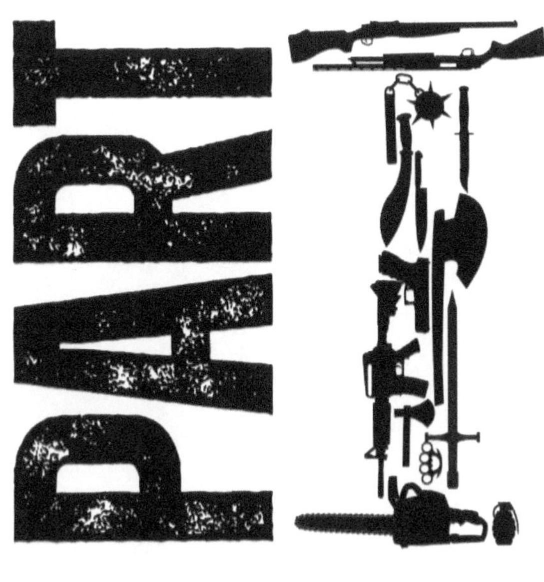

PEOPLE OF THE RED NIGHT

WRITTEN BY

JOSH POWELL

1

Bare feet scrambled across pavement, leaving blotches of blood on the yellow dashes of a dark, silent road. The panicked, flailing twenty-something man wore only a pair of ill-fitting, black dress pants and was covered in cuts, bruises, and blood from head to waist. With empty grass fields on either side of the road, his desperate, wheezing gasps were the only sounds around. The road's end could not be seen from his vantage point, but he couldn't stop moving. Whatever was behind him was far worse than anything the darkness of night could reveal.

Headlights emerged from the distance ahead of him and grew in size as he continued running.

"Oh my God," the man gasped.

The man waved his hands as he hurried forward.

"Help me! Help me, please!" the man yelled, illuminated by the headlights.

The Mercedes-Benz E 350 slowed as it reached the man and came to a stop. The man darted to the driver's side window.

"Please! You have to help me! Get me out of here!" The man spoke so close to the window that he fogged the glass.

The driver was a stocky, bald, sixty-something man in a button-up shirt, accompanied by a forty-something woman in a luxurious dress. Both of them were frozen in confusion and couldn't respond.

The bloody man pointed in the direction he came from and screamed, "People are trying to kill me! Please, call the police!"

The driver tried to speak but could only open his mouth and let out a startled breath as the woman beside him patted his shoulder.

Inside the car, the driver finally said, "What in the great hell?"

"Harry, leave him," the woman screeched with a trembling voice. "We'll call somebody. This isn't our business."

Though her voice was muffled, the bloody man could still make out the remarks.

"No, no, Harry, sir, please! Please, help me!" the man shouted as he placed his hands on the window, leaving bloody smears.

"Ah, Jesus!" the woman shouted, pulling out her phone. "The hobo got blood on your car. Drive away, honey."

"I need help! My name is Jackson Dawkins. I escaped, and they'll come for me."

"Jesus," Harry said. "Honey, call the cops. Kid's in rough shape."

"Yes, yes, call the cops!" Jackson pleaded.

The woman dialed 9-1-1 and put the phone to her ear, then said, "Harry, don't you let him in this car."

Harry cracked the window open just enough to be heard clearly and said, "Just hang on a minute, son. We'll get this sorted out."

"Thank you! Oh God, thank you!"

The bloody man listened as the woman spoke into her phone. "Yes, hello. My name is Lucille. My husband and I came across a man on the road, and he looks hurt real bad. He's real bloodied and bruised. Never seen anything like it around here. We're on Mead Street heading toward the Brighton Heights neighborhood ... Yes, and he said ... Oh, God, um, he said people are trying to kill him ... Okay, yes, I can stay on the line."

She muttered to Harry, "They're sending someone."

Harry looked over to Jackson and said, "The police are on their way—"

Harry was drawn to headlights ahead of him. Jackson looked over and saw that an SUV was speeding towards them.

"Shit! They're coming!!" Jackson yelled. "Don't let them take me back, please!"

Harry reached for the unlock button just as the woman slapped his arm and yelled, "Do not let that man in this car!"

Harry saw the fear in Jackson's eyes. He reached over to the glove box and pulled out a Glock.

"Just hide behind the car for now," Harry ordered Jackson.

Jackson hurried around as the car slowly pulled off the road and settled. He ducked down on the side of the car farthest from the road and whimpered to himself, watching the growing shine of the headlights envelope the Mercedes.

Then ... a low, guttural growl sounded near Jackson. He swung his head around to view the source of the animalistic noise but could see nothing in the darkness.

"Jackson," an impossibly deep voice vibrated around Jackson like a droning, pulsing synth.

His eyes searched through the night to find the source of the sound.

"You musssssst bring us more," the disembodied voice rumbled.

Jackson pushed his quivering body against the car and shielded his ears.

"No, no, no, no," Jackson whispered to himself.

On the other side of the Mercedes, the SUV came to a stop on the opposite traffic lane. The vehicle was all black with tinted windows, nearly invisible under the faint moonlight.

Inside the Mercedes, Harry clutched the handle of the Glock.

"I'm scared," Lucille whispered, the phone still glued to her ear.

"Everything'll be fine, honey," Harry said through gritted teeth, his eyes trained on the SUV.

"A black SUV just pulled up," Lucille said into the phone. "How long is it gonna take for someone to get here? ... Hello?"

Lucille looked at the phone, then murmured, "The call cut out."

The SUV's driver's side window lowered to reveal a handsome middle-aged man in a white, button-up shirt and bowtie. The man smirked and waved to Harry.

Harry slowly reached towards the window controls and lowered his window.

"Hey there," the man said, keeping his smile as wide as could be. "Car trouble?"

"Uh, yeah," Harry said. "Something like that."

"Need a hand?"

"Ah, thanks for asking, but we got help on the way."

"Well, that's good news," the man said. "Hey, so, my name is Patrick and I'm out looking for someone. Uh ... My cousin came to visit and he's not doing too well. He had a bit of an episode tonight. I guess you could call it a mental breakdown. He attacked some of my dinner guests and ran off. You wouldn't by any chance have seen a guy in his early twenties on this road?"

"Oh, that's horrible," Harry said. "Uh … Did you call the police and tell them about it?"

"I thought I'd try to find him myself first. I'm afraid they'll send him away. He's a good kid, he's just really troubled."

"Oh," Harry started, thinking of the right words to say. "Is he dangerous?"

Patrick smiled slyly, then said, "I noticed you have a bit of blood on your car."

Harry froze … then squeaked out, "Oh, yeah?"

Patrick let out a deep breath. "What did he say to you? When he gets like this, there's no telling what'll come out of his mouth."

"We called the cops," Harry said. "They'll come and sort everything out."

Patrick's smile faded as he said, "Where is he?"

Harry didn't answer.

Lucille tapped Harry on the hand and whispered, "Honey … I don't like this."

Patrick opened his car door and stepped onto the pavement.

"You, my friend," the man snarled, "have created an unenviable situation."

Harry lifted his gun-wielding hand and pointed the barrel at Patrick.

"Don't come closer!" Harry said with a shaky voice. "We'll wait for the police to get here."

Patrick halted and studied Harry for a moment.

"That's cute," Patrick chuckled.

The other three SUV doors opened, and three men in black suits joined Patrick, each with their hands over the sidearms at their hips, sweating profusely, anxiety all over their faces.

"Stop!" Jackson's screech sounded from the other side of the Mercedes. "Get out of my head! Get out of my head! What did you assholes do to me?!"

Jackson could be heard bashing his head into the side of the car. Harry and Lucille looked over their shoulders with worry, then looked at each other with uncertain eyes.

"I told you," Patrick said. "He's very sick. And he needs to come with us right now."

Harry stared up at the men, the gun trembling in his hand.

"Just what the hell is going on here?" Harry mumbled.

The tension was broken by sirens in the distance. Harry looked at his rearview and saw a squad car speeding towards them.

"Goddammit," Patrick said under his breath, then turned to the other suited men and said, "I'll handle this."

"You damn well better," one of the men snarked.

The squad car reached the scene and stopped as Patrick prepared his biggest smile yet. Everything within view was blasted with flashing blues and reds as a gruff officer in his fifties stepped out of the car.

Patrick raised his hands and said, "Thank God you're here, officer. There's been a wild misunderstanding."

Jackson darted from behind the Mercedes straight towards the officer.

"Help! Help me, please! Those men are trying to kill me!"

The officer shielded Jackson behind his body with a hand on his sidearm and looked at the suited men in bewilderment.

"Yeah, see, that right there ... *That* is the misunderstanding," Patrick said with a soft laugh.

Harry slowly opened his car door, returned his gun to the glove box, and held his hands up as he rose and stood beside his car.

"Officer, my wife made the call," Harry yelled out. "We came across that boy running for his life. Then these men showed up saying he's a cousin and he's crazy, and now ... Now, we don't know heads or tails."

The officer scoped out the scene as Jackson quivered behind him. He looked over his shoulder to view Jackson.

"Good God," the officer muttered to himself.

The officer turned back to the group and said, "Okay, here's what's gonna happen. I'm gonna call in an ambulance for him while I get statements from everyone."

"Yes, sir," Harry said.

Patrick called out, "I assure you, Mister ..."

"Hodge. Officer Hodge."

"Officer Hodge," Patrick said, "I assure you that's not necessary."

Hodge sent a cold stare at Patrick. He kept his eyes on Patrick as he slowly ushered Jackson to the back of the squad car and opened the door for him.

"Thank you, officer," Jackson said with tears in his eyes.

Hodge looked down at Jackson with a stone-cold demeanor that flattened Jackson's excitement at the thought of a potential rescue. Hodge reached into his right cargo pants pocket, pulled out a pair of black gloves, and slid them on, fitting the leather atop each finger meticulously. He robotically turned to the men illuminated by the array of lights spraying out of the squad car, and Jackson noticed a worn, black handle of a pistol protruding from Hodge's belt at his lower back. Jackson's body tingled with chills. Was this a rescue, or the continuation of his waking nightmare?

"Officer Hodge," Patrick said. "Maybe it would help if you knew the man I'm associated with."

Hodge stood there a moment observing the scared-shitless Harry and the gang of sleazy well-dressed men.

"I know who you're associated with," Hodge said as he swung the car door shut on Jackson. Then Jackson faintly heard the officer tell them, "You've been eliminated."

The officer drew the pistol from his back and sent a bullet through Patrick's neck.

BANG! BANG! BANG!

Hodge lit into the suited men, sending them crashing to the ground with holes in their chests. The men struggled to grab their pistols to return fire, desperately gasping for air. He stormed them and double-tapped them one by one.

Harry was on his knees shielding his head, gunsmoke wafting around him. Hodge picked up Patrick's fallen pistol and turned his attention to Harry.

"Harry!" Lucille called out from inside the car. "Oh, God, Harry, are you okay?!"

"I ... I ... I'm okay, honey." Harry kept his eyes on the pavement, too afraid to look up.

Hodge's boots trotted over to Harry and stopped just inches from him.

Harry slowly peered up and saw that Hodge was still firmly clutching his pistol. Harry looked into Hodge's eyes and saw no compassion.

A soft, "Sir?" was all Harry could manage.

"I'm sorry," Hodge said, tightening his grip on the gun at his hip.

"Sir ... We ... We've done nothing wrong."

"Tonight, you entered into a world where there is no right or wrong. Only win or lose," Hodge said through clenched teeth.

Jackson watched from the police car's caged back seat as the officer pointed his gun down at Harry.

POP POP!

Jackson viewed Harry flop lifelessly onto the road. Lucille's screams pierced the sky until—

POP POP!

Bursts of blood filled the car, and the screams ceased. Hodge looked down the road in each direction, then jogged to Patrick's corpse, and put the pistol in his hand. Hodge shifted over to the Mercedes, picked up Harry's pistol, and shot a round into each slain man. He placed the gun next to Harry.

Jackson sobbed at the realization that the waking nightmare would continue.

"I can't go back," he cried out to himself. "Don't take me back there."

The metal surrounding Jackson bowed out and settled back to normal like elastic. A warping synth accompanied the bizarre occurrence.

"Jackson," The ethereal voice reverberated through the squad car.

Jackson shoved his hands over his ears and screamed, "No! Get out of my head!"

"You musssssst bring us more. We ... are ... sssssss ... so hungry."

The voice chanted at Jackson, repeating the phrase over and over until the officer opened the door and the voice ceased. Hodge settled into the driver's seat and shut the door. The officer stayed quiet as Jackson cried into his hands.

"Sorry, kid ... Once you're in, there's no way out."

2

Richie was running away from the shadow of his family, but the track was composed of quicksand. The object in front of his eyes should have elicited the greatest sensation of joy he had ever felt, but it instead served as a reminder of just how heavy life had become, and he was carrying that weight on a sore back.

He finally realized that the smile on Kate's face had faded behind the pregnancy test she had raised to him.

"Do you think this is bad?" she murmured.

He feigned a smile and shook his head.

"No, honey. It's just ... You caught me off guard is all. This is ... Wow ... This is great news."

He saw that her eyes didn't fully believe him, but he didn't know how to hide his fear of the situation. He wrapped his arms around her and placed his cheek on hers, hoping the right words to say would come to him.

They were both twenty-three years old, working paycheck-to-paycheck to afford a one-bedroom apartment while chipping away at a mountain of debt they weren't sure they'd ever get over. Nearly a year ago, Richie was the victim of a hit-and-run that totaled his car, spiked his insurance, and sent him into back surgery. The three months that Richie missed work while recovering nearly resulted in eviction, but Kate hustled to get as much overtime as she could at the nursing home to keep them treading water. Just weeks after Richie returned to his home renovation job, their apartment was burglarized while they were both at work. He had pitched to Kate that he might be cursed, a thought stemming from a childhood where he witnessed his brother overdose, his mother disappearing, and his father wasting away in a cloud of drugs, alcohol, and crime. His father wanted to mold Richie to be his partner in chaos and nearly succeeded, but after near-death experiences selling drugs, a stint in juvie, and discovering love with Kate, he vowed to do absolutely anything to be nothing like his DNA.

But ... why was an inch always a mile? Why was an accomplishment always followed by a devastating setback? Why did he have to be terrified that he was having a child with a woman he loved so dearly?

Kate slowly pulled away from him to say, "I was worried to tell you. I know it's not a great time for us. And if you think it's too much, we'll weigh our options."

"Well, how do you feel?" he asked.

"I feel ... scared. I feel ... excited. I feel like it's gonna be hard. It's something we've said we wanted, but ... not this soon, right?"

Richie studied her eyes for a moment. She couldn't help but wear her emotions loudly on her sleeve. She wanted this.

"I ..." He started, but stopped.

"Talk to me." She softly placed her head on his chest.

"I want you to have everything. And I want to have everything with you. It's just ... Nothing ever works for us."

Kate lifted her head to meet his eyes and said, "Hey. I believe in you. And I believe in us. So, I don't wanna hear about curses or bad luck. We have each other and that's pretty lucky."

Richie smiled at her. "I am pretty damn lucky."

Kate beamed up at him. Richie kissed her on the forehead.

"From now on," he placed his hand on her stomach, "we make our own luck. And I'll do anything to make sure you and this little one are safe and comfortable and happy."

She smiled and kissed him softly, then looked into his eyes and said, "Yeah, we make our own luck. I like that."

She eased out a heavy breath of anxious excitement. "So we're really doing this."

He grinned and nodded to her. She jumped him and straddled him with excitement.

Richie walked out into the apartment complex's parking lot with a thermos full of coffee and a head full of doubt. He eased into the barely-clinging-to-life '02 Toyota Camry he bought after his accident, which came loaded with several unenviable features, including stains on every seat, nicotine-flavored air conditioning, and a passenger's side door that could only be opened from within. He looked at his phone screen to check the time, but was met with a grim notification: *Email - Bill Overdue*. He dropped the phone in the passenger's seat and wiped an uneasy hand over his face.

Just remember ... We make our own luck.

He slid the key into the ignition and twisted only to hear the pitiful squeal and halting of a dying engine. He twisted the key again, and the car whimpered awake.

The house the crew was working on was in a suburban cul-de-sac surrounded by three-story homes that looked like mansions to Richie. The homeowners hired the company because they "needed an addition" to their house. When Richie heard that, the sarcastic thought almost came out of his mouth, '*Of course, with a house this big, who wouldn't need ... a bigger house*'. The plus side of this job was that the homeowners were out most of the day. Nothing worse than being talked down to by a work-from-home investment banker with a small-dick insecurity or a drunk housewife in need of unleashing her frustration on someone beneath her. Richie had spent years working on the short temper that got him into bad spots in his teen years, and wealthy assholes presented him tests of how far he had come with his anger management.

Working for people he despised as much as they despised him and helping them add to their collection of excessive possessions was never a part of the plan. The plan was to stay sober, work hard, learn from the company's rags-to-middle-class CEO Dan Tiggins, and save up enough to start his own home renovation business. Richie wasn't book smart, but he could work harder and longer than anyone around him. With the debt he had accumulated recently, saving up had become impossible. But he couldn't give up, especially not with a baby on the way. After all, he wasn't his father. He had made the decision that he would soon talk to Tiggins about a step up in responsibilities and, in turn, a step up in pay.

When the crew broke for lunch, Richie wanted to stay behind and keep working. His brain was so wired with thoughts about the future. Doing a task he didn't have to think too hard about but could see through to the end was a small success he needed on that day. The hulking team lead, Marcus, told him he'd bring him back a burrito after he told him to not put a nail through his hand while they were gone. They drove off as Richie was taking a nail gun to a two-by-four. The sequence of 'POP-POP-POP, move, POP-POP-POP, move' was the familiar repetition he needed to ease his mind.

It wasn't ten minutes before Richie's peace was interrupted by the sound of an engine roaring into the driveway of the house. From the side of the house where he was working, Richie could see a shiny black sedan with curves and angles that made it look sporty and expensive. A man in his forties stepped out of the car in a suit that was tailored to be snug on his athletic build. He was growling into his phone at some poor soul catching wrath.

Great ... The rich, small-dick-insecurity homeowner came back early. Richie put his head down and got back to work.

Five minutes later ... "Howdy." The man broke Richie's peace once again.

Richie eased the nail gun off the two-by-four he was tending to, and replied, "Hello."

"Where's everybody else?" the man asked.

"Out to lunch."

"They didn't care to take you with them?"

"I wanted to work."

"You wanted to work through lunch while everyone else took off?"

"Well ... I don't like to leave a job unfinished."

The man laughed. "That's crazy. You know it's about a hundred degrees out here?"

"I like the heat."

The man smirked as he stepped forward, extended his hand, and said, "Aiden Prince."

Richie shook his hand and said, "Richie."

"Oh, I don't get a full name, Richie? Come on, man, we're professionals."

Richie smirked. "Richie Stull."

"Alright, Richie Stull," Aiden said, releasing Richie's hand. "I appreciate your work ethic and your attitude."

Richie nodded to him and said, "Thank you, Mr. Prince."

"Call me Aiden, my friend. So, Richie ... wife and kids?"

"Girlfriend. Well, more like a life partner. Known her since middle school. And actually ... Just found out we have one on the way."

"Wow, no kidding? You just found that out?"

"Yeah, she told me this morning."

"That's huge! Congratulations, Richie."

"Thank you, I appreciate that. I don't know how I'll make it work, but ... I'll make sure I do."

Aiden looked at Richie a while, like he was studying Richie's aura, all while keeping a glowing white smile one could never get through natural means. Aiden then looked all around at the addition Richie was working on and nodded at Richie with admiration.

"Big opportunities are coming your way, Richie Stull," Aiden said. "I know it. Just be open to them when they present themselves."

"Oh ... Yeah ... Okay. I'll keep that in mind," Richie said.

"Well, I gotta hop on a call," Aiden said. "But it was great chatting with you, Richie Stull."

"Likewise," Richie said.

***

Around five o'clock, Richie and the other crew members packed into a pickup truck and drove a half-hour back to the double-wide trailer that Tiggins conducted business out of. Richie stepped out onto the dusty dirt field, hoping to find the confidence to ask Tiggins for a bump up.

Diego grasped Richie's shoulders with a smile and said, "You wanna grab a beer to start the weekend off right?"

"Man, I'd love to, but I gotta spend some time with Kate."

"Uh oh. Trouble in paradise?"

Richie laughed. "Nah, not at all. Only good stuff. Just on boyfriend duty."

"Ah, I know all about that, my man," Diego said with a chuckle.

They all halted when they finally noticed Tiggins slumped over in a chair outside the trailer with a nearly empty bottle of whiskey in hand.

Marcus called out to Tiggins, "Boss? You doin' alright?"

Tiggins lifted his head with a somber expression. "You want the truth on that?"

"What's goin' on?" Marcus responded as the team gained on Tiggins.

Tiggins looked up at the men standing in front of him with a quivering chin and said, "We're done."

Silence overtook them, until Marcus broke it. "What you mean, Boss?"

Tiggins dropped the bottle of whisky and wiped his mouth with his sleeve.

"I got nothing," Tiggins said. "We're deep, deep in the red. I can't pay y'all past this week. We can't finish any open projects. I failed. I failed all y'all."

Richie watched in disbelief as a roughneck who built a business on blood, sweat, and tears, a man he held in such high regard, a man whose path he wanted to follow, shed tears of regret.

Then it hit Richie.

What the hell was he going to do now?

"Goddammit!" Diego shouted out. He was diminutive but was never one to keep his mouth shut. "Tell me this is a joke."

Tiggins picked up the whiskey bottle and took a swig, then responded, "Ain't a joke. I'm sorry."

"You're sorry?!" Diego growled. "My wife can't work right now. This paycheck is all we have!"

"I'm sorry," Tiggins muttered again.

"All you got is sorries? That's all you got right now?!" Diego stepped toward Tiggins. and Marcus cut in front of him.

"Hey, now. Don't do anything you'll regret," Marcus said.

Diego backed away and turned around with his hands grasping his head.

Tiggins peeked up at Richie but quickly looked away. He knew how much Richie looked up to him, and it was just too much to look Richie in the eyes.

Another setback.

Quicksand.

Richie clenched his fist as he looked down at the pouting, defeated man, waiting for him to crack a laugh and reveal that this was all just a bad joke. But that moment never came. Tiggins just kept his head down and moped like he was waiting on the dirt he was staring at to transform into a hole that would swallow him down. Richie placed a hand on Tiggins' shoulder and crouched down to come face-to-face with him. Even with Richie directly in front of his eyes, Tiggins refused to meet Richie's gaze. Richie's grip tightened on Tiggins' shoulder, a silent fury coursing through Richie's entire being.

Richie released Tiggins and trudged to his car without even realizing that Diego and Marcus were barking at each other coming close to blows. The other two crew members had already gone to their cars without putting up a fight.

Richie eased into the driver's seat; the world stood still around him. The air was stale and thick. He couldn't miss even a day of work. They needed to bring in as much money as possible to prepare for the baby. Then, once the baby was born, they'd have to look for daycares. But, the high cost of daycares might force Kate to stay home and take care of the baby. But, how could they keep an apartment on only one paycheck? A paycheck that at that moment, Richie had no idea where it would come from. Would they be forced to face the tough decision of not having the baby? Would he prove to be a failure just like his father?

A series of knocks on the driver's side window snapped Richie out of his existential dread. It was Diego, huffing with bubbling anger. Richie rolled down the window, allowing a waft of furious hot breath to flow into his face.

"So," Diego uttered among heavy exhales. "How do you feel about that beer, now?"

Richie knew he shouldn't drink in that state of mind, but he couldn't go home and tell Kate the news immediately. A little liquid courage might help. On the way to the bar, he called Kate and told her that was getting a drink with "the guys" and would be home late.

"What's the rule?" she asked him in a motherly tone.

"Don't do anything stupid," he replied.

"And if you're about to do anything stupid?"

"Call you any time."

"That's right," she said. "Have fun, babe."

It was a fair warning given Richie's history of drunken bar fights, but Kate couldn't have known how important that reminder was given recent events. He figured one beer with his buddy to help calm his scurrying thoughts would be good for him. He wouldn't let one turn into two, then three, then four. Just one. Maybe two for good measure. But that's it.

The Dirt was the only bar in a fifteen-mile radius, and the name certainly sent a clear message about what to expect for all who entered. The walls had old cigarette smoke stains, the pool sticks were held together by duct tape, the floor was so sticky that it might claim your shoes, and who knows how much mold the patrons were exposed to. Richie and Diego were slumped over the bar, a few silent patrons to their right and left, and a rowdy group of burly men behind them playing pool. The first few sips of cheap, not-cold-enough beer didn't provide quite the relief Richie was hoping for, so he kept drinking in hopes that relief would come. Three beers didn't do the job either. When he took the last sip of his third, Diego was already pounding back his fifth.

"That bastard," Diego said with a slur, repeating the same things he'd been spewing for the past two hours. "Not even a warning. How do you just fuck over your people like that? Just goes to show, you can't never get too close to anybody. Can't trust no one in this world."

"Tough pill to swallow," Richie said.

"I don't know how I'm gonna tell the wife. Shit, at least I didn't *lose* a job this time around. Just had a lousy boss."

"Kate's pregnant."

Diego backed away for a moment and looked at Richie through half-closed, glazed eyes.

"Holy shit," Diego said, cracking a smile. "You're joining the dad club, man."

"I'm scared as hell," Richie let out.

The group of men playing pool behind them howled like dogs and shoved each other with happy tough-guy energy. Obviously, every place they entered was theirs, and everyone else had to endure their idiocy. Richie ignored them, but Diego couldn't continue without a snide comment.

"Fat fucks," Diego muttered to himself. The remark was tame considering the colorful shit Richie had heard spew from Diego's mouth.

Diego went on, "Hey man, you'll find a way. When my kid was born, I shoplifted, I begged, I made an ass out of myself, but I made it work. You're a better man than me. Shit, it would be sad if you weren't. You'll make it work."

Richie nodded to him, though he didn't fully believe that sentiment, then said, "You got any idea what you'll do for work?"

Diego didn't get a chance to answer as a thick and musky body inserted itself between them.

"Another round over here," the man mumbled through a thick beard covered in glistening beer dew and small chunks of, well, some kind of deep-fried shit.

"Ay!" Diego shouted up at the man. "What the hell's your problem?"

The man looked down at Diego and grunted, "Huh?"

"Huh?" Diego scoffed. "We're having a conversation here. You mind?"

The man raised his eyebrows sarcastically, looked over at Richie, then turned back to Diego.

"Y'all on a date?" the man said, and a smirk started to form under his wires.

Diego clenched his jaw, chuckled, then slowly rose to meet the man face-to-face.

Richie could see where this was headed. Hell, it was an exchange of dumb, rhetorical questions by sweaty cave men disrespecting personal space; anyone could see where it was heading. Truth be told, Richie would've loved a fight at that moment. Getting lost in a flurry of fists and blood caused a high that no drug or drink he tried could ever touch. But he had to think about Kate. He had to think about his new role as a father figure. He had to prove to himself that he had matured into a positive force.

"Hey," Diego said directly into the man's face. "This ain't the night. And I ain't the guy. Get lost, okay?"

As Diego and the man continued to square each other up like boxers at weigh-in, Richie rose, placed a hand on the man's shoulder, and said, "Hey, we're good here."

The man didn't acknowledge Richie behind him, and instead, cracked a smile at Diego and inched closer to him, almost tapping noses.

"Oh, yeah?" the man said. "Why don't you tell me what kinda night it is. And tell me what kinda guy you are."

Richie walked around from behind the man, put a hand on Diego's chest, and said, "This isn't worth it tonight, D."

"I wanna know what he has to say," the grizzly man demanded as he shoved Richie out of the way.

Richie backpedaled into a high-top table, sending half-drank glasses of beer crashing to the ground. Diego sent a wild, retaliatory swing at the man's jaw and connected with a harsh *CRUNCH*. The man recovered and tackled Diego to the floor as the man's two friends darted in to help pummel a dazed and belligerent Diego.

In heightened moments of intense adrenaline release, Richie experienced the actions within his surroundings slow down to a fraction of their normal speed. It had been that way since he was a kid. It's what made him good at sports, great in emergency situations, and downright dangerous in fistfights. At fifteen, he fought with Danny Harris in pouring rain and watched Danny's knuckles burst through raindrops before dodging the punch. He didn't know if this was something other people experienced or if this was a unique ability, like some kind of superpower.

With a burst of adrenaline, Richie viewed the men rush Diego ... bar patrons looking on with worry ... Diego squirming on the bar floor in a daze ... a fist plunging into Diego's gut ... a boot ramming into Diego's ribs.

Richie's jumping heart was sending ripples through his jacket. Nothing else mattered. There was no world outside of this moment. All there was ... was fight.

Richie stormed the men and sent a haymaker into the cheek closest to him, then grabbed a handful of greasy hair and forced his fist into a snout. Knuckles appeared directly into the middle of Richie's tunnel vision and drilled him in the jaw. Richie spun around, regrouped, and laid eyes on the man who rang his bell, a man who had no idea of the devastation coming his way if he didn't stay down after the next punch. Richie spat blood into the man's face, stunning him, then clocked the poor bastard in his front teeth. The man stumbled backward, crashed into the bar counter, and flopped onto the floor beside Diego. Richie offered a hand to Diego but caught a flailing fist in the eye that forced him to a knee. In a blind rage, Richie shouted like a man possessed and propelled himself up with an uppercut to the assailant's chin, sending the man flailing backward, slipping on spilt beer, and potato-sacking the floor.

"You dumb shit." The bearded man grunted, stumbling to his feet, wiping blood from his lip. "That's how you fight? You sucker punch people who ain't lookin'?"

Through untameable panting, Richie responded, "I'm lookin' at you, right now."

Richie had no idea when exactly he made contact with the man who kicked the whole thing off. Richie was a bull who saw red, and all three men were the same color. Apparently, he hadn't hit the lumberjack quite hard enough, but he was happy to give it another shot.

The man ripped his jacket off of his barrel-chested torso, spit blood on the floor, and mumbled, "You just got you and your friend hurt real bad."

The man lumbered towards Richie, every muscle in his body flexed, pounding the ground with every step.

Richie didn't wait. He charged the man and powered his fist into the man's nostrils before the man could even lift his hands to prepare. Richie felt the tip of the nose crunch into the man's skull, forever altering the man's future headshots and family photos.

A burst of blood spewed from the man's upturned face like a fountain as he spun and crumpled.

Richie rocked on his feet above the three downed men and Diego with loud, furious breaths. Diego wobbled to his feet, still in a daze. There was an eerie silence through the bar, as all eyes were on Richie like he was a dangerous zoo animal. The slow world gradually quickened as Richie caught his breath. Soon, Richie could see everything clearly, and, quite clearly, he had made a damned bloody mess. He wiped his palm across his lips, brought his hand to his eyes, and saw red. He lifted his eyes to the fifty-year-old, white-mustached bartender, who was frozen in place.

"Son," the bartender murmured. "You'd better go now."

Richie helped Diego out of the bar and drove him home. In return for helping Diego get home safe, Richie received Diego's drunken, concussion-induced cries of embarrassment and worry. Richie watched Diego stumble over dead grass on his way to the front door of his dilapidated house. Diego reached for the nob but keeled over and vomited into a dead potted plant at his feet. A totally defeated Diego rested his back against the door, sat there under the fluorescent porch light, and waved Richie away. He wasn't signaling that he was okay, but rather that he didn't care if he was okay or not. *Fuck this night and leave me alone.* Richie was on the same sorry page.

The stillness of the apartment complex parking lot didn't help Richie in organizing a game plan for the remaining hours of the night. How would he break the news to Kate about his unemployment? He didn't want to cause her stress ... She was pregnant for God's sake. He would certainly hit the ground running first thing in the morning and find a new job, and this would prove to be a small bump in the road. But, what about his curse?

No. Fuck a curse.

We make our own luck.

Maybe, just maybe, everything would work itself out.

Just as morale was on the up, Richie caught a glimpse of himself in the rearview mirror.

A black eye. A swollen lip. Dried blood crusted on his chin.

Damn. He looked like hell. He was either attacked or he engaged in a brutal brawl, and Kate would easily discern which. Richie's heart plummeted into his stomach with the realization that the trust he had earned from Kate would be sullied. Perhaps even worse, the trust he had built within himself was shot. He wasn't between a rock and a hard place; he *was* the rock in a hard place.

Richie eased through the apartment door and was greeted only by the dim kitchen light and silence. He slugged to the bedroom where Kate was sleeping soundly. He sat on the side of the bed and placed a hand on her cheek, keeping his face turned away from her so as not to reveal his battle scars. Kate stirred awake and placed her hand on his.

"Babe," she mumbled with a groggy throat, her eyes barely open. "You were gone so long."

"I'm sorry," he whispered. "Diego had a lot to get off his chest. He drank too much. I ended up having to take him home."

"That's sweet of you. You smell like work. Take a shower and get in bed."

"Yes, ma'am."

Richie's wet hair matted against his eyes as water pelted his head. His showers were usually short, but he was making this one last. He washed the blood from his chin, but there was no hiding a blackened eye and puffy mouth. In the morning, he would have to explain to Kate that he was defending Diego from a belligerent band of assholes. Though, under no circumstances could he reveal to her the sheer euphoria of causing large men intense pain with his bare fists. More importantly, under no circumstances could he share with anyone that he receives an unmatchable jolt of ecstasy when his flesh and bones are damaged in a fiery exchange of blows. Who would understand?

A ringtone took him out of his steamy daze as his phone rang on the counter of the vanity. The sound was an odd carnival-like jingle he had never heard come from his phone. He cut off the shower, threw a towel around his waist, and snatched the phone to see a number he didn't recognize. He silenced the call and put the phone down. He took the towel off and wiped it across his waterlogged face.

The phone rang again. The same jingle. The same number.

This time, Richie answered.

"Hello?" Richie said.

"Richie Stull?" a voice asked.

"Yes?"

"This is Aiden Prince. We met earlier today."

"Oh ... Oh ... Yeah ... Hey, Aiden."

"Sorry to call you so late, but you made an impression on me, and I was hoping we could meet for lunch tomorrow."

"Tomorrow? Um ... Yeah ... Yeah, I don't see why not."

"Great. It'll be worth your while, Richie Stull."

3

The big-ass dark spot around his eye and the swollen lip hadn't magically disappeared overnight. Throw in the obvious crusty, red damage to his knuckles, and there was no way to hide that he had gotten into a scrap. He didn't even try the whole *'you should've seen the other guy'* shtick, because, as good as it felt to ruin some punchable faces, the shame he felt from losing control overshadowed the knockouts. A nightmare of fists careening towards him from a void of darkness forced Richie to awake atop soggy sheets around four in the morning. He managed to avoid waking Kate as he made a pot of coffee to sip in silence.

When the sun rose, so did Kate, and the calm morning she thought was ahead immediately took a dive out the window.

"Are you hurt? Is anyone hurt? What were you thinking?" Kate ran through questions like a game show lightning round as she hovered her hands over his face, careful not to make direct contact.

"Some assholes started something up with Diego," he said through a narrow mouth.

"And you finished it?" She scoffed with disappointment. "You finished it. Right, of course you did."

"I tried to stop it before it started. They rushed him. It was three-on-one, and I jumped in."

"Jesus. Did you hurt anybody bad?"

"I might've. Didn't stay around to check."

Kate paced around the kitchen, shaking her head, and said, "You're gonna have to go to work on Monday looking like that."

Oh ...

Richie didn't respond. He wasn't ready to spill the rough news. Not yet.

"Do I need to be worried about you?" she asked him with a bold stare.

Richie kept quiet and lowered his eyes. He wanted to be re-assuring, but that question was more loaded than Kate realized. Kate took Richie's silence as self-shame. A teardrop welled up in Richie's good eye and landed on the table below his face. She shuffled over to him, sat beside him, and grabbed his hand.

"Hey," she whispered. "I'm glad you're okay."

She gently placed her hand on his cheek and said, "I like this face. I need it to be out of harm's way."

Richie nodded to her with a forced smirk.

"And I know what you're like when you fight —"

Richie interjected, "I know ... I know."

She leaned in and softly kissed his swollen lip.

"How's that feel?" she asked.

Richie grinned and said, "Always good."

Kate smiled and made her way to the coffee pot.

"Hey, I got something to tell you," Richie muttered.

"What's that?" she asked, pouring herself a big cup of coffee.

"I uh ... "

"Yeah?"

Luckily, Richie happened to remember some other, lesser important news that could help him stall on the big, bad, more relevant news.

"Oh, yeah, um," Richie started. "A guy wanted to meet me for lunch. He owns the house we were working on last week. Got to chatting with him yesterday."

"He wants to have lunch with you?" she asked after a sip. "What do you think he wants to talk to you about?"

"Not sure. But, he said he liked my work ethic. Said I made a good impression or something."

"Huh." She sat down next to him. "Interesting."

"I don't know. Maybe he has freelance work for me. Or, maybe he just thinks I'm a cool guy."

"Oh, the coolest guy." Her playful sarcasm had no subtlety. "But, have you looked at your face? You want me to put some makeup on you before your big date?"

He chuckled at her and gave her a playful shoulder shove.

On the drive to the restaurant, the confusion of why Aiden would reach out to him had transformed into hope. Aiden had told Richie to be open to new opportunities. Could it be that Aiden was foreshadowing a life-changing opportunity? Hell, even if the wealthy, slick-haired smooth-talker had the lousiest of opportunities, Richie was in no position to take anything off the table. He had to go into this lunch meeting with the same confidence he had planned to unload on Tiggins.

Then, Richie caught his reflection.

Damn. What a fuck-up.

Richie pulled up to a hotel holding the Capital Grille on the first floor. This was exactly the type of fancy restaurant Richie always scoffed at. *Why would anyone get a fifty-dollar steak when they could get a five-dollar burger?* Though he found the place pretentious, and though he wanted to exude confidence to Aiden, he walked in with his chin down so as not to draw attention to his battered face. Aiden hopped up from a table in grey slacks and a white dress shirt so tight Richie could nearly see his toned abs through it. Aiden was undoubtedly the best-looking man in the establishment, with obvious attention paid to his quaffed hair, flawless skin, and dapper style. With a beaming smile, Aiden waved Richie over, light reflecting off of Aiden's silver-rimmed sunglasses in his shirt pocket. Richie shuffled to him, head still craned down just a bit, as if there was any world where he could actually hide the markings on his face at all.

"Hey, there he is!" Aiden shouted with no care to whom he was disturbing.

Aiden took Richie's hand with a firm grip and a vigorous shake.

"Ah, shit," Aiden got a good look at Aiden's face. "Richie, that's quite a shiner you got there. What the hell happened?"

"Went for a drink after work and some guys jumped my buddy," Richie responded. "I stepped in to help. To be clear, I tried to stop it before it started, but ..."

"Ah, so it's a 'you should see the other guys' type situation, huh?" Aiden cheesed.

"Well ... they picked a bad night, I guess."

"Then I would love to see the others." Aiden gave Richie a tough pat on the shoulder. "Well, sit down, man. Let's get some food. Hope you're hungry. And don't even look at the prices, it's on me, my friend."

Aiden ordered them calamari, wine, and thick slabs of juicy steak. He asked Richie about his upbringing, about what "forged that work ethic." When Richie gave a short answer and turned the spotlight back onto Aiden, Aiden wasn't shy. The man knew how to talk an ear off. He told Richie his life story, from a lower-middle-class, single mother upbringing, to a three-sport star athlete, to a college scholar, to quickly working his way up the corporate ladder. Aiden claimed to have figured out "the game" and knew how to play it. *What game was Aiden speaking of? The game of life, maybe?* Aiden spoke like an expert but was vague enough to force your mind to aggrandize. But it was far from a one-sided conversation. When Aiden spoke of his childhood and his accomplishments, he was boisterous, and when he gave Richie the floor, he was quiet and attentive. Amidst all his bravado, he seemed genuinely interested in what Richie had to share. Aiden had a balance of confidence and curiosity that Richie had never encountered.

"So, you like where you work?" Aiden asked, chomping on a cut of pink steak.

"Oh, well ..." Richie mumbled. "So, I guess you haven't heard yet."

"Heard what?"

"I don't know if it's my place to say."

"What are you talking about? I'm not following."

Richie let out an uncomfortable sigh before starting, "When we got back to the office yesterday, we were told that the company tanked. We're done. Just like that."

Richie lowered his head in dejection.

"Damn." Aiden leaned back in his chair. "The job's not even half done. Guess I gotta chase him down to get my money back."

"Sorry, I figured Mr. Tiggins would've told you. Maybe he was planning on telling you on Monday—"

"Hey, come on, you don't have to apologize. You weren't running the show, even though you probably should've been."

"Well, thank you. I mean, I could finish it up for you. I could see if Tiggins would lend me the truck and tools. You'll spend less money paying one man, and I'd still get it done by the same deadline."

Aiden chuckled as he lifted his wine glass and sipped.

"Ya know," Aiden said, "It doesn't surprise me one bit that you would say that, Richie Stull."

Aiden stared at Richie with a wide grin, making eye contact for an amount of time that Richie was uncomfortable with but endured, hoping to appear professional.

"I believe you." Aiden finally broke the silence. "You're a 'how high?' kind of jumper. You're the type of guy that'll work till his fingers bleed. I got that right?"

"Yes, sir. Absolutely," Richie said with an assured nod.

"And now you got a baby on the way."

"... That's right."

"In a most vulnerable moment in a man's life, the world snatches away the man's ability to provide. Life is ... quite a beast, isn't it?"

"... Yeah ... Life is a beast."

Aiden smirked. "The beast is tameable with the right tools. Which brings me to this ... You're probably wondering why you're sitting across from me right now."

"The thought crossed my mind," Richie said with a slight chuckle.

"It's because I'm a great judge of character. It's a skill that has helped me build a great life for myself and my wife. I see a lot of potential in you. You have determination, you have skill, you have strength, you have love in your heart, and ... at this moment in time ... you have the ultimate incentive to make things work. That, my friend, is the ultimate cocktail for a big swing. Now, life ... this 'beast' we're talking about ... it sometimes plays favorites and leaves more deserving people behind. Do you sometimes feel as if, no matter how hard you try, things just don't go your way? Like ... when something great happens, something horrible is bound to follow?"

Aiden was speaking directly to Richie's soul.

"Quicksand," Richie whispered.

"Quicksand? ... Hmm. Yeah, Quicksand." Aiden nodded with acknowledgement. "But that black eye tells me that you don't take shit lying down, right?"

Richie smirked. "I can't go down. Not without a fight."

"I like that." Aiden smiled at Richie in admiration, then leaned in. "Listen, I'm going to a networking event tonight. A lot of people are looking for young, ambitious people like yourself. I'd like you to come with me."

Richie eased back into his chair with confusion. "Um ... you want me to come to some corporate, businessy meet-and-greet?"

"That's right."

"Um ... Yeah, I'm sorry, I just, um ... I've never pictured myself in a setting like that. I mean ... I went to a cousin's wedding in a polo shirt I borrowed from the cousin who was getting married."

"Let me fill you in on a secret. The corporate world is a mess right now. The younger generations on payroll are obsessed with work-life balance, mental health breaks, extra PTO to take vacations, and, mind you, the vacations aren't meant to be enjoyed; they're photo shoots for some fake social media presence. That's not to mention the nepotism, the entitlement, the coddled children who think sending an email is a hard day's work. The people at the top salivate for hardworking young adults. People who have endured real hardships. People who know what it's like to struggle and fight to survive. People who work when the rest of the team is checked out. People who have this inherent will to finish the job."

Aiden looked around and leaned in, as if he was revealing a secret. Richie instinctively craned his head forward.

Aiden whispered, "The true titans of industry understand the value of struggle. Without struggle, we create boogeymen for ourselves, invisible obstacles, diagnoses, worries, concerns, fear of the dark. With struggle, you learn to not fear the monster, but become the monster slayer. The business world is burnt out on Ivy League frat boys who seem lost without a breast to suckle. Titans seek gladiators. And, Richie, that's why I want you to accompany me tonight."

Richie studied Aiden's stern boulder of a face and felt the man's intensity radiating like a heat wave. Everything Aiden said made complete sense, almost as if he had reached into Richie's head and grabbed a handful of thoughts. Richie knew that this wasn't a promise of something better, but it was exactly what he needed ... an opportunity. An opportunity to prove that he was more than where he came from, more than a former juvenile delinquent, more than a mountain of debt, more than a magnet for bad luck, and more than his father's expectations.

"So, what do you think, Richie Stull?" Aiden whispered with a toothy smile.

Richie couldn't help but grin as the thought raced its way to the front of his mind ...

We make our own luck.

Richie nodded to Aiden. "When and where?"

Aiden enthusiastically reached his hand out to Richie and said, "My man."

Richie grasped Aiden's hand with a firm, assertive shake.

Through a pleased smirk, Aiden said, "Meet me at my place at seven."

4

A trip to the thrift store was an easy sell. Kate loved un-earthing unique threads at the bottom of a clothing pile and transforming them into a standout wardrobe piece. But Richie was never the one to initiate such a trip. Richie hated shopping, especially for himself, so if he actually wanted to get a new outfit, Kate knew it must be important.

"So … this … random guy …" Kate began to prod, watching Richie sift through second-hand blazers.

"Aiden," Richie said without looking.

"Right. Aiden. So, this random guy Aiden wants you to be his plus one to some … 'networking event'?"

"Yeah. Pretty wild, right?" Richie chuckled.

"It's just … this friendship seems to be escalating pretty quick, don't you think?"

Richie peeled his attention off of clothes, turned to Kate, and sighed with frustration.

"Come on," Kate said with an eye roll. "The day after you meet a guy twice your age, he treats you to lunch, then asks you to come to a rich people party?"

"He seems like a nice guy who sees something in me."

"I just …" Kate didn't know how to finish.

"Why are you being so weird about this?"

"It just seems like," Kate looked left and right to make sure no one else was in the aisle to hear her, " ... I don't know ... some kind of grooming."

"Grooming?" Richie leaned into Kate to get a feel for just how serious her statement was.

"Yeah, babe," Kate whispered. "Maybe a weird pyramid scheme that preys on young, ambitious people. Maybe cult shit. Maybe sex cult shit."

"Sex cult?" Richie said, just a little too loud, forcing Kate to shush him.

"It sounds crazy, but—"

"Kate," Richie cut her off. "You think maybe you've been watching too many true crime shows?"

"Stop," Kate snipped. "It just seems a little out of left field. And I don't want you to get taken advantage of by some sleazebag."

"I understand. But, is it so crazy to think that something good could happen for me? That something good could happen for us? It does seem strange, I get that. But I'm not scared of walking into a strange situation, then ditching a strange situation. I'm scared of passing up a good situation."

"... Well ..." Kate still wasn't quite convinced.

"What did we promise each other?" Richie asked. "We make our own luck, right?"

Kate bit her lip with apprehension and eventually mumbled, "Okay. But you better be careful tonight."

"Yes, ma'am." Richie embraced her. "Any cult activity, or nudity, I'll rush home immediately."

Kate playfully pushed him away. "Damn right. Now, let's get you looking good."

With Kate's help, Richie settled on a pair of khakis, a white button-up shirt, and a black tie. Each item was just a little too large in certain areas. The pants didn't hug his leg like Aiden's pants. The shirt wasn't flush on his arms or midsection like Aiden's shirts. The tie was bulky, unlike Aiden's slim ties. But it was the best they could find, and Kate said he looked "like a damn snack" with wanting eyes practically undressing him. At least Richie knew that, even if the event didn't go well, Kate would be excited to greet her sharp-dressed man when he got back home.

"You wearin' this home or what?" Kate said with a sly smile.

Richie playfully shook his head, unknotted the tie, and removed it with a swift woosh. "One step at a time."

Richie looked himself over in the bedroom mirror garbed in the khakis and white dress shirt, an image that seemed alien to him. He always felt uncomfortable in what others deemed as "nice clothes." He grabbed the black tie off the counter and looped it around his neck. His first try ended in the tie hanging far too short. The second try, comically long. Luckily, the third try was interrupted by Kate.

"If you need something done right," Kate said as she took control of the tie. "Ask a woman first."

"Shouldn't be so hard," Richie uttered. "Should've got a clip-on."

She giggled as she said to herself, "And loop, and pull."

She backed away and studied him. She bit her lip and raised an eyebrow.

"So ... " she whispered through pouty lips. "Think you could be just a little late?"

Richie grinned and shook his head. "Cut it out."

"Just sayin'." Kate wrapped her arms around him and moved in, nose-to-nose. "You clean up good. And I hate to admit it, but ... the black eye ... it's kind of working for me."

"The black eye? Really?"

"Must say. Speaking of, this guy didn't care about your very obvious black eye at all?"

"Um ... I actually think he dug it," Richie said. "I think he likes that I'm not afraid to stand up to someone. He gave me this whole speech about how the world's gone soft and businesses are looking for fighters and survivors. Something like that."

"I really hope they don't rope you into becoming a door-to-door vacuum salesman or something," Kate said.

Richie playfully backed away from her and said, "Okay, okay—"

"I'm done, I promise." She shifted forward and clung to him. "Just be careful. You don't know this guy, and you don't know what you're walking into. I don't know how long you'll be gone. I'm allowed to be nervous."

"I know." He pulled her into his chest and slowly swayed side-to-side with her.

He lowered down to his knees so he could directly address Kate's stomach.

"Hi there," Richie said. "I'm your dad. I would love to spend more time with you, but I need to go to this thing tonight. You're in safe hands. Please, remind your mom throughout the night that I'm fine and there's no need to worry. Please, tell her that I will text her and keep her updated. Thanks, young one. You're the best."

Richie rose back up to see Kate blushing bright red.

"I'll let you know if she says anything about you while you're gone." Kate teased.

"It's a girl?"

"Oh, I have no idea."

"Hm ... I could be a girl dad."

Kate beamed and laid a big kiss on his lips.

The taking-it-a-day-at-a-time sedan screamed "I don't belong here," zagging through Aiden's gaudy neighborhood. Richie remembered the way to Aiden's home, which featured the bare bones of an additional room with an unknown future completion date. *Whoops.* Though one of the three-car garage's doors was open, and the driveway was empty, Richie parked his hunk of metal at the curb in front of the freshly cut lawn. He looked in the rearview mirror, tried to look past his bruised eye, and centered his tie. Was he ready? Well, he was a twenty-three-year-old who barely graduated high school, a laborer by trade, with a penchant for beating the hell out of people, dressed in hand-me-down khakis, accompanying a slick fast-talker he barely knew to a networking event. He was as ready as he'd ever be.

Walking up the driveway, he was halted by Aiden yelling out the front door.

"Richie, buddy, don't be silly. You're welcome company. Park in the garage."

"Oh," Richie mumbled. "Yeah, okay. I can do that."

Richie eased the struggling car into the garage, like dollar store ramen noodles inside fine china. He was parked right next to Aiden's sparkling sports car, which was next to a gargantuan SUV. The garage door closed behind Richie as Aiden walked out with a pep in his suave step, donning skin-tight dark blue pants and a pink, open-collared dress shirt.

"There he is!" Aiden pointed at Richie with an ear-to-ear smile.

Aiden's handshake vibrated Richie's entire body.

"This'll be a great night," Aiden pronounced. "Are you excited, my friend?"

"Can't wait," Richie responded with a smirk.

"Beautiful. Well, come inside for a second." Aiden placed a hand between Richie's shoulder blades to guide him through the house, passing by large paintings of confusing abstract art, into the immaculate (seemingly unused) kitchen, and into a living room with a sectional sofa that could seat an army.

"I haven't quite settled on a tie yet, and my wonderful wife isn't being helpful at all ..." Aiden looked over his shoulder to shout, "Isn't that right, honey?"

Aiden paused as he waited for a response, creating a new layer of uneasiness that made the foreign space seem even more foreign to Richie. When Aiden finally gave up on receiving a reply, he chuckled, turned back to Richie, and said, "She's great. Would you mind hanging out for a second? I'm sorry that you have to witness one of my fatal flaws. I must admit, I worry about my appearance quite a bit. Maybe to an unhealthy degree."

"Oh, no, I don't mind at all," Richie said. "I'll wait. No problem."

"My guy." Aiden smiled and strutted away.

"Oh, honey," Aiden snarked into the air. "Please, greet our guest and offer him a drink. Thank you."

"Oh, I'm fine—" Richie started.

"She'll be out soon," Aiden said before disappearing down a hallway.

Richie looked around the living room, from the glistening hardwood floors to the TV spanning nearly the entire wall. It was more of a movie theater than a living room. An adjacent wall featured large black-and-white photos of a woman in the nude striking sensual, commanding poses. *Giant pictures of a naked woman in your living room for all to see?* Before Richie wasted too much thought on it, he chalked it up to ...

Rich people shit.

He took a seat on the couch and ... damn. For the first time in his life, his ass and back felt the kind of comfort that "fuck you" money provides. Richie's brain turned off as newfound pleasure overcame him, leading to an audible moan.

"Well, hello." A quiet, sultry voice greeted Richie.

Richie nearly jumped up from the couch and cleared his throat. There was Sofia, late-thirties, statuesque, and olive, in a sparking low-cut dress clinging to every toned curve, sipping from a wine glass as she sauntered her way over to Richie. It took him all of two seconds to realize that she was the nude woman in the giant pictures. He tried to ignore the part of his brain reminding him in big, bold letters that he knows what she looks like completely naked. It didn't help that her pursed lips, subtle smirk, and piercing stare, creating a feeling of a reverse growth spurt, shrinking him inch by inch.

"So, the couch is quite comfortable, yeah?" she said with a slight slur.

"It's um ... yes. Very." Richie flubbed.

"You moaned a bit there."

"Ah. So, you heard that."

She smiled with levity. "I thought it was funny. Would you like a drink?"

"I think I'm okay right now. Thank you for offering."

"Never underestimate the power of alcohol to help us through the discomfort of reality. What's your name?"

"I'm Richie." He offered his hand.

"Sofia." She shook his hand softly, which was welcome after all of Aiden's earthquaking shakes.

"Make yourself comfortable," she said, gesturing to the couch. "You can even make more noises if you'd like."

Aiden laughed as he sat back down. "Ah, I can't live that down, can I?"

Sofia caressed Richie's shoulder as she shuffled passed him and eased into the sectional across from him. She crossed her legs and took another sip of wine.

"You like what you see?" she asked.

"Um ... I'm sorry?"

"The house."

"Oh, oh. Yeah, it's pretty amazing. You two are very lucky."

"Oh," Sofia scoffed. "It's a big thing that holds smaller things. We have rooms that are literally empty. Doesn't make much sense, does it?"

"Um ... I guess not."

Sofia's smirk faded as she studied Richie. Her demeanor turned from playful to firm, turning Richie's palms to swamps.

He broke the silence. "So, you're going with us tonight?"

"No, I'm not."

"Oh, I just saw the dress ..."

"Tonight, I have the house to myself, and I'm dressing up just for me. I'm nobody's arm candy, nobody's accessory, just me ... just for me. And I'll be getting wine-drunk, of course."

"I see." Richie didn't quite understand, but didn't dig any further.

"What are you looking for, Richie?" she asked.

Richie thought about it. "Right now? Just ... opportunity, I guess."

"An opportunity for a better life?"

"I guess so, yeah."

Sofia ceased eye contact with Richie, instead focusing on her glass of wine. She took another sip, this one bigger than the last.

Without looking at Richie, she said, "A man down on his luck happens upon a door erect in the forest. He opens the door and sees that it leads to a dark tunnel, so dark he cannot see to the other side. The desperate man has a choice to make: Close the door, knowing there are endless possibilities at the end of the tunnel, or walk through the door with the hope that there is a light at the end of the tunnel. With the latter option, the man mustn't allow himself to dismiss one inscrutable fact: The tunnel is dark."

Richie looked at her with bugged-out, uncomfortable eyes.

"Funny, isn't it?" she spoke as if she were lost in her own world. "How you can reach the better life you were hoping for, only to realize you would be happier with worse?"

Richie felt large rocks of discomfort on his shoulders. "Ms. Prince ... Are you okay?"

Sofia popped her head up and smiled in a flash.

"Wow," she giggled. "I must've zoned out there."

"Oh, that's okay," Richie said with a shiver down his back.

They sat in silence for a moment. *How could she be unhappy in a place like this?* It was a question he truly wanted to know the answer to but was far too timid to ask.

Aiden's voice boomed through the living room, "Sofia, my love."

Sporting a floral skinny tie over his pink shirt and a slim, dark-blue jacket matching his pants, Aiden speed-walked to Sofia and kissed her on the lips.

"Amazing, isn't she?" Aiden said before grasping his nose, wrestling it side-to-side, and snorting.

"We had a great talk," Richie said.

"Oh, was she saying bad things about me?" Aiden cackled. "I'm joking, I'm joking."

Aiden looked down at Sofia and said, "We must be going now, my dear."

Sofia nodded to Aiden with a false grin and looked into Richie's eyes.

"Richie," She spoke quietly, as if it were just the two of them in the room together. "I truly wish you ... the best of luck."

Richie saw the genuineness in Sofia's eyes.

"Thank you, Ms. Prince."

Aiden chuckled as he strolled over to Richie.

"We'll have a great time, my love," Aiden declared, hovering behind Richie with his hands on Richie's shoulders. "Richie here just found out he's going to be a father. I *have* to show him a good time."

Richie rose from the couch with a big grin as Aiden patted his back with cheesy enthusiasm.

"Is that so?" Sofia murmured.

Richie looked over to Sofia and saw that she wasn't joining in the joy. Instead, she was frozen in place with a pale look of intense worry.

"Um ..." Richie started. "Yeah."

Sofia turned her tense gaze to Aiden.

The ever-smiling Aiden spoke as if the palpable tension was nonexistent. "Isn't that great, honey?"

Sofia shifted her eyes back to Richie. Her whole body was clenched like she was captive.

"Ms. Prince?" Richie said.

Sofia forcefully raised one corner of her mouth, then the other, to form an unnatural, almost painful smile. She rose up from the couch and took another shaky sip of wine, finishing off the glass. She opened her mouth to speak, but nothing came out, not even a breath.

"Honey?" Aiden said, keeping his smile intact. "Is everything okay?"

Sofia's chin quivered. She staggered a bit.

"I ..." Was all she could let out.

Richie felt her eyes locked onto him and cocked his head, wildly perplexed.

Sofia swiftly turned and walked away, soon out of sight within the massive home.

"Hon?" Aiden called out.

"Is something wrong?" Richie asked.

Aiden leaned in and whispered, "She has a tendency to hit the bottle a bit too hard. And she has a weak stomach. She'll be fine. We should head out."

"Do you wanna check on her?"

"Oh, trust me, I know her too well. She's probably embarrassed. It's best to give her some space right now."

"Okay ... Okay, if you say so."

Aiden lifted his head away from Richie and hollered, "Call me if you need anything, my love!"

Aiden then gestured toward the direction where they entered. "Shall we?"

5

A never-ending playlist of classical music flowed through the silent, squeaky clean sedan cabin. Aiden claimed that classical music was "the music of the thinking man." All Richie could think about was the horrified look on Sophia's face and Aiden's nonchalance towards it.

"Hey, buddy, can you hear me?" Aiden finally broke through to Richie.

Richie rattled his head around and said, "Wow, sorry. I just got a little zoned out there."

"I get it. It got weird back there."

"Oh. You mean with—"

"It's okay, you don't have to play coy. Look, I don't like to tell people this, but I feel like I can confide in you. Can I confide in you, Richie?"

"Yeah. Yeah, sure. I mean ... yes, you can."

Aiden turned the music down a few decibels. "She hasn't been the same since we realized we weren't able to get pregnant. That's why your news, as amazing as it is, it brings up really painful feelings."

"Wow, I ... I'm really sorry—"

Aiden smirked as he said, "Buddy, you apologize too much. You did nothing wrong. It's just still a bit of an open wound for her. You understand."

Richie gave a nod. "I do."

"Thanks for being cool about it." Aiden turned the music back up. "You're one of the good ones. So, tell me more about what you want from life."

The long drive allowed ample time for Richie to cover all the details he hadn't yet revealed to Aiden. His desire to prove to himself that he could be better than the template provided by his family. His worries about his ability to provide for his partner and child. But also, his conviction that he would do anything to make sure his child had a loving and stable upbringing. Even if it meant he worked till his hands and feet bled, he would do anything to take care of his family.

"Anything?" Aiden asked.

"Anything," Richie said sternly.

Aiden took his eyes off the road to look at Richie. "You really mean that. Don't you?"

Richie stared back into Aiden. "Yes sir, I do."

Aiden smiled ear-to-ear as he slowly turned his head back to the road. "Love it. I love it."

***

The sun was stubborn but had finally begun its descent, blanketing everything in a red glow. They had travelled past farmland and empty fields before reaching an eight-foot-tall stone wall, the narrow road leading to a behemoth metal gate.

"Pretty pretentious, huh?" Aiden scoffed.

Richie chuckled and said, "Wouldn't know. Never seen anything like it."

Aiden slowed to a stop beside the gate's standing key code panel and punched in a combination that emitted well over ten beeps. Whatever the code was, it was long as hell. With a grinding squeal, the gate began to ease open. Aiden swung his head over to Richie and hiked his eyebrows a few times.

"Exclusive shit," Aiden said with a smug grin. "We're in the jungle now, baby."

Richie was too mesmerized by the giant gate and the massive houses it revealed to pay any attention to Aiden's "cool-guy" shtick. The neighborhood was as picturesque as an old Hollywood movie with a modern architectural flair. Massive houses of steel and glass, manicured lawns, perfectly round bushes, expensive cars, identical trees, men in khakis watering plants, women speed walking in pricey athleisure to burn some calories just before darkness descended. Even the dogs being walked seemed to carry uppity condescension. Aiden gave two-finger waves to everyone they passed as Richie looked out the window like an astronaut discovering an alien world.

The neighborhood street led to yet another tall, iron gate. That's right ... A gated house within a gated community. A cursive "B" was embedded across the vertical bars. Another ten-plus-digit code triggered the gate to open.

"The Brenadeir Estate," Aiden announced.

Elegance. Luxury. Wealth—No ... This was beyond wealth. The place Richie laid his eyes on was the kind of thing folks make a deal with a devil to get. At least, that's the only way his brain could make sense of it. The pavement circled around a gaudy fountain fronting a full-blown mansion with countless doors, windows, and balconies. The driveway hosted dozens of sports cars and SUVs. Richie's heart raced at all of these unfamiliar sights, so out of his element, so anxious that he was worried his legs wouldn't work well enough to carry him to the front door. An immaculately dressed muscular man with a shaved, veiny head stood in front of the front door with his hands clasped in front of his waist. Aiden parked next to a purple space-ship-looking two-seater car.

"Show time." Aiden patted Richie on the chest, bringing Richie back to reality.

Richie looked at Aiden with wide eyes.

Aiden chuckled. "It's crazy, right? Mr. Brenadeir's a good guy. He worked hard for all of it. See, this ..." Aiden pointed to the home in admiration. "This doesn't happen by luck or accident."

Richie was far too gobsmacked to interact with Aiden's idolatry.

"It's a lot to take in, huh?" Aiden said.

"How ..." Richie finally found words. "This is ... insane. How ... How do you know this guy?"

"My mentor has a mentor, who has a mentor, who was mentored by Mr. Brenadeir. Quite a web of success stories. I have to do right by the men who did right by me, that's the deal. And I do that by providing opportunities to young people who have a burning fire inside of them. Your fire isn't just burning, young man. It's raging. There are business leaders in there who are gonna wanna meet you. I know it's probably a bit overwhelming, but just follow my lead. I won't steer you wrong."

Aiden winked at Richie, then exited the car. Richie followed suit and walked on wobbly legs and stone feet beside Aiden. They came to the buff, suited monster at the ten-foot-tall wooden double-doors, and Aiden planted himself in front of the man with his head high.

"Red night," Aiden said to the man.

The man nodded to Aiden, then held both his hands out to them, and muttered, "Phones."

Aiden was quick to place his phone in the man's hand.

"Wait," Richie directed to Aiden. "We have to give up our phones?"

"Security purposes," Aiden responded. "Some people in there don't want their pictures taken or their conversations recorded. It's standard practice."

"Um ..." Richie thought for a moment. "I told my girlfriend I would update her through the night."

"Oh, Richie, my friend, I'm sorry I didn't tell you sooner. It's a strict guideline here. If you must, you can come outside, grab your phone, and update her. But phones are strictly prohibited inside. And, to be honest, this area has rough cell service anyways."

Richie looked at the doorman's massive outstretched hand. He pulled his phone from his pocket and checked the screen. Just as Aiden said, there was bomb-shelter-like cell service. Richie thought it over with deep breaths.

"I can assure you, we won't be here all night," Aiden said. "This is business, not pleasure. What, you can't last a little while without your phone?"

Aiden put a reassuring hand on Richie's shoulder.

"Eh, maybe I can last a few seconds without it," Richie said with a smirk.

"A few seconds? Woah, don't hurt yourself," Aiden said with a cheesy cackle as Richie handed his phone to the doorman.

The man stepped aside.

"Thank you, my large friend." Aiden nodded to the man.

Aiden led the way and nudged the wooden doors open.

6

The sounds of Beethoven floated through Richie's ears as he followed Aiden inside to a mammoth room dimly lit by a chandelier hanging from an impossibly high ceiling and lanterns lining the rustic, wooden walls. There were hallways on each side, large double doors at the other end of the room, and staircases on either side that led to an overlooking second floor. A sea of well-dressed men ranging from forties to seventies were mingling with glasses of dark liquor and wine in hand atop pristine tile. Women of the same age range in Kentucky-Derby-style outfits were sprinkled here and there, far outnumbered but carrying the torch of bold fashion. Scattered in the sea were a handful of twenty-something men and women dressed in "as-good-as-I-can-do" clothes. Fortunately, Richie wasn't the only sore thumb sticking out.

The doors shut behind Aiden and Richie with an echoing thud, causing several eyes to shift in their direction.

"Aiden Prince!" A cheerful, bowling ball of a man hollered through a white goatee, clutching a glass of bourbon.

The man waddled his way over as Aiden called out, "Ah, Mr. Quinn. How the hell are ya?"

Aiden offered an emphatic hand, and Mr. Quinn shook it like thunder.

"Let me guess," Mr. Quinn cheesed, showing every unnaturally shiny tooth in his mouth as he continued to maul Aiden's hand. "You had trouble getting out the door because you were worried about your outfit."

"Hey, come on, now." Aiden laughed with rolled eyes. "It was just the tie that I second-guessed. The rest of the fit, I quite like."

"Oh." Mr. Quinn looked Aiden up and down. "You sure about that, Prince?"

Aiden put his hands on his stomach to highlight his belly laugh. "Always bustin' balls, Mr. Quinn. Always bustin' balls."

Mr. Quinn looked over to Richie. "Hey now, if you're hangin' around Prince, not sure if I trust your judgment."

Mr. Quinn let out a wide-mouthed, mucusy cackle, and Aiden joined him with a pat on Mr. Quinn's shoulder. Richie looked between them and forced a confused, half-hearted laugh.

Aiden gathered himself. "Mr. Quinn, this is Richie Stull. I met him just yesterday, and he left quite an impression. He's a hard worker with a good head on his shoulders."

Mr. Quinn offered his hand to Richie. "Jonathon Quinn. Pleasure to meet you, Richie."

Richie shook the meaty, sweaty hand. "The pleasure is mine, sir."

"What's your line of work?" Mr. Quinn asked.

"Well, right now—" Richie was interrupted by Aiden.

"Home renovation. Kid's as tough as the nails he hammers." Aiden nodded to Richie.

"Ah, home reno, huh?" Mr. Quinn said. "Working with your hands out in the heat. You don't mind a hard day's work, do ya, Richie?"

"No, sir," Richie said. "The harder, the better."

"I love it. You look like you can take a punch, kid." Mr. Quinn motioned to Richie's black eye.

Aiden butted in. "He can throw one, too."

"Oh, no," Richie chimed in to save face. "This here was, um ... It was an accident."

Aiden chuckled. "Richie's being modest. He took down a whole gang of drunken assholes to protect his friend from getting the hell beat out of him."

Mr. Quinn lifted his brows at Richie. "Is that so?"

Richie slowly nodded. "Yes, sir. Wish it hadn't gotten to that point, but—"

"My, oh my." Mr. Quinn smiled as he patted Aiden on the shoulder. "I like this one, Prince. Well done. You two go get yourselves a drink and mingle."

"Will do, Mr. Quinn," Aiden said as Mr. Quinn grinned and walked back to the crowd.

"Quick tip," Aiden said into Richie's ear. "Don't drink. Stay sharp."

Richie looked at Aiden as Aiden winked at him. "Got it."

"Come on." Aiden guided Richie with a hand on his back. "A lot more folks I want you to meet."

Aiden sauntered chest-first towards the crowd with Richie at his side. As they moved, Richie made eye contact with a moppy-headed twenty-something in wide, navy dress pants and a collared shirt, having a hard time concentrating on a group of hyena-like suited men. The two looked at each other for a while with the same thought ... *What the hell are we doing here?* The guy gave Richie a subtle nod, and Richie sent one back.

"Hey boys, look what the cat dragged in." A raspy-voiced, stocky man in a grey, tailored suit opened up a spot in a circle of scotch-drinking neanderthals wearing pricey threads and wide grins.

"Andruzzi, ya ol' bastard." Aiden shook Andruzzi's hand and slapped him on the shoulder.

"Old?" Adruzzi shot back with a smirk. "Maybe I should take you a few rounds in the ring so you can see what a real man's hands can do."

"Watch out, now. I got back up." Aiden motioned to Richie. "Don't make me sic 'im on you."

Andruzzi looked to Richie and stuck his hands in the air. "Hey, I surrender."

The circle broke out in over-the-top laughter, which Richie was already on the verge of growing tired of.

"George Andruzzi." The man held his hand out to Richie.

"Richie Stull, sir." Richie shook the man's hand and immediately realized that this type of full-name, crushing handshake meet-and-greet would be the thing he would tire of first.

"And what's your story?" Andruzzi inquired.

"My friend Richie, here," Aiden began, "has a great work ethic and a real fighting spirit. He'd run through a wall if he had to."

"Oh, uh." Richie let out a nervous laugh. "I don't know about that."

"No room for modesty here, Richie." Andruzzi gave Richie's arm a squeeze and nodded to himself. "A fighter's mentality'll do ya good. And ... I think I might just see that in your eyes. You can always tell by the eyes."

Richie stood still as he felt multiple sets of eyes on him. "Well ... thank you, sir. I'm hoping to learn."

"And," Aiden spoke up, "Richie here got news that he's going to be a father. How about that?"

Andruzzi took a step back and put a hand on his chest. "That is quite the news. Congratulations."

"Thank you, sir," Richie responded.

Andruzzi eyed Richie from head to toe and back to head.

"Richie ... Richie ... Yes." Andruzzi reached into his jacket pocket, pulled out a black business card, and handed it to Richie. "We must discuss business."

Richie took the business card and saw that it was simply a plain, black rectangle. No text, logo, or website. Just a small piece of thick stock paper showing zero details.

"I'm sorry, sir," Richie said. "You must've given me the wrong card. There's nothing on this."

Andruzzi grinned. "Make sure you keep it safe."

"Um ... yeah, okay."

"He certainly will," Aiden interjected. "We're going to make the rounds, gentlemen. Enjoy your night."

Aiden guided Richie away and whispered to him, "A black card from George Andruzzi. Wow. That's a good guy to have in your corner."

"What's the deal with the card?"

"It's a sign of interest. A pretty exclusive sign of interest."

"There's nothin' on it."

"That's right. This crowd doesn't offer personal details to people they don't know. A black card shows that if they want to know more about you, they'll contact you. It's a big deal to get a black card. You should be proud of yourself, my friend."

Richie's eyes floated to a man in a grey suit with olive skin and a stagnant forehead. The Botox was doing some serious work keeping the wrinkles away. Too much, Richie would say, for a man who wasn't even forty yet. He didn't follow politics too well but knew from social media who Congressman John Stallings was, though he couldn't name the state he represented. All Richie knew was that the man was a Christian Nationalist Republican and embroiled in a scandal involving alleged sex with a minor. And the woman standing next to him in a suit jacket and long skirt—*Holy shit,* Richie couldn't believe it—was Congresswoman Jennifer Parsons, a Democrat who had gone viral sparring with Stallings over a bill to defund education.

Richie said to Aiden, "Are those two who I think they are?" He pointed with his chin, careful not to draw attention to himself.

Aiden laughed. "They most certainly are."

"They should hate each other, shouldn't they?"

"Makes you wonder, doesn't it? Whether the political game, the finger pointing and name calling, is all bullshit clickbait?"

From afar, Parsons tilted her head back in a laugh, nearly spilling her drink, and placed a hand on Stallings' chest.

"It sure does," Richie said.

Aiden's focus shifted to a fedora-wearing seventy-year-old man with his hand around a tan fifty-something woman with lips close to bursting from filler.

"Mr. Cordova, handsome as ever!"

Small talk. Shitty jokes. Shit-eating grins. Black cards. The repetition was enough to drive most people mad. Names and faces flew at Richie like baseballs at a batting cage. He had no way to gauge his effectiveness in these interactions, no way of knowing if he was making a good impression on these bigwigs, and no way of deciphering which of the many strangers were genuine when they complimented him. Of course, these compliments, ranging from "sharp as a tack" to "having the 'it' factor", were based on nothing more than a handshake and a quick visual. Richie had a decent bullshit meter, and that meter skewed toward bullshit more often than not based on a general distrust learned from life experience. But this was a different world. Brand new territory. Richie knew he had to check his biases at the door for a seat at the table, whatever that would eventually mean. Scanning the decor, the clothes, the gold rings, the flashy watches, the affluence ... Richie was willing to play the game.

Still, no matter how much he tried to will himself to feel differently, Richie was uncomfortable. The myriad of loud, obnoxious men was an attack on the senses. Richie needed a break to recuperate.

"Hey, Aiden," Richie tried to speak over a knee-slapping laugh Aiden was sending to a Mr. Jacobs, or Jameson, or Jetson, or whatever-the-hell.

"Yeah, buddy, what's up?" Aiden leaned over to Richie.

"I'm gonna hit the bathroom real quick."

"Gotcha." Aiden pointed to the left corner of the room. "Just down the hall that way. Hurry back. Mr. Brenadeir should step out any second."

"Okay. Will do."

Richie walked away from Aiden and zagged through the chatty socialites.

"Well, look at you," he heard a slurring mid-fifties woman in a glorious, feathery dress mumble as he passed by.

"Hello, ma'am," Richie said as he continued on. He couldn't help but smirk. Maybe he had enough charm to hide the fact that he was completely out of his comfort zone.

A dark hallway of illuminated paintings led to a bathroom door. Richie peered at the paintings as he walked by, each one featuring a white man with whiter hair either posing by himself or engaging in hunting with rifles and large dogs. This had to be Mr. Brenadeir or the lineage of proud Brenadeir men.

Richie walked through the door at the end of the hall to see the moppy-headed guy he'd locked eyes with earlier washing his hands in a multi-stall event-style restroom.

"Hey, I clocked you when you walked in," the guy said. "Glad to see someone else with that deer-in-the-headlights look, I gotta say."

"The headlights are bright out there." Richie walked past him to a urinal.

"You're tellin' me. I've been washing my hands for the last ten minutes to get away. I don't know what the hell I'm doin' here. I'm Tyler, by the way."

"I'm Richie. How'd you get invited?"

"A guy I met when I was visiting my mom in the hospital. Started asking me some questions. Told him I dropped out of college to work full-time and help my mom pay for her medical bills. And those bills are crushing us. Long story short, he said I'm a good candidate."

"A good candidate for what?" Richie asked.

"Still trying to figure that out. The guy works in investment banking. Pretty sure everyone I've met here works in investments, or commercial real estate, or comes from a long line of people who make big money. Why would they be interested in sussing out someone like me? Not quite sure. You got any ideas?"

Richie zipped up his pants, flushed, and replaced Tyler at the sink. "Maybe it's some type of power trip for them. Maybe these guys get off on finding some wild card proteges from out of left field and molding them into versions of themselves."

"Hmm ..." Tyler thought for a moment. "It's a rich-people game. That's not bad."

Richie wiped his hands with an embroidered white cloth from a stack of identical rags. "Have you met anyone else here who's ... ya know ... like us?"

"Just briefly," Tyler said. "I met Wade. He's a six-foot-four gym rat, so he's hard to miss. He's in the company of the undoubtedly alcoholic Mr. Phife. And I met Helena. Black dress. Combat boots. Dark eyes. She wasn't much of a talker, but Mrs. Vanderloo sure thinks highly of her."

Richie pulled four black cards out of his pocket and showed them to Tyler. "You got any of these?

Tyler laughed and grabbed a card from his pocket as well. "All black. No text. That's some rich people shit if I've ever seen it."

Richie smirked. "How much longer you gonna hide in here?"

"Eh," Tyler said. "Maybe it's time to venture out there and put on my schmoozin' face. These people are out-of-touch, condescending douche bags, but if they can get me a decent job, then whatever."

Tyler lightly slapped his cheeks and made a wild, exaggerated smile at Richie.

"How's my schmooze face?" Tyler said through his teeth.

"Wow. So authentic."

Tyler chuckled and opened the door. "After you."

Richie and Tyler walked down the hall of hunting portraits.

"You know when this is supposed to be over?" Richie asked.

"No idea," Tyler said as he grimaced at a slain deer in a painting. "I guess we're waiting to see this Mr. Bermuda or whatever his name is."

Richie looked at his wrist in hopes that a watch would somehow appear. His watch was his phone, which was in the pocket of a Schwarzenegger clone. He was anxious to update Kate on the weirdness of the night, and, more importantly, to let her know he was alive.

They turned the corner and were right back in the shuffle of the crowd. Tyler was immediately spotted by a suave silver fox with one hand holding a glass of whiskey at his chest and the other hand resting in his pants pocket.

"Hey, hey, there he is," the man said as he moseyed over, oozing calm and cool.

"Hello, Mr. Crow, sir." Tyler immediately put on a wide smile and altered his voice to sound just a bit more business-like. "I'm quite sorry I took so long. I got to talking with Richie here. Salt of the Earth, this guy. Salt of the Earth, indeed."

Mr. Crow gave Richie the full-body scan that seemed to be the norm with these people.

"Richie." Mr. Crow smirked slyly as he talked. "If I'm not mistaken, you have a child on the way."

"Um ... yes. Yes, I do."

"Word's been getting around about you, young man." Mr. Crow took a sip from his glass.

"Oh?" Richie wasn't quite sure what to make of it. Surely, there were things to highlight about him in the context of a networking event other than his impending fatherhood.

"Well, well," Tyler cut in with the same over-the-top act. "All press is good press, as they say. I'm just glad I can make a new friend in a place as unlikely as a bathroom. Life sure is something."

Mr. Crow chuckled. "It's great that you two are hitting it off. Friendship is something I've learned to be quite wary of. When the chips are down, you don't know who will cross you. But what hurts even more, you disturb yourself with who you're willing to cross ... and what you're willing to do for your own preservation."

Richie laughed off the remark, but the more he and Tyler eyed Mr. Crow, the more they realized just how dead-serious he was.

"Alright," Tyler broke the silence. "Thank you for the, um ... advice?"

Mr. Crow slowly moved his eyes right and left, studying both of them for an uncomfortably long period of time.

"Hey, Crow," Aiden's voice snapped the tension as he juked through the crowd toward them, careful not to spill his drink. "Don't go corrupting my buddy here. He's one of the good ones."

With a wide grin, Aiden slapped Mr. Crow's back.

Mr. Crow clinked his glass to Aiden's and said, "This world corrupts us all at some point."

Aiden shook his head at Mr. Crow. "Oh, so dour."

Mr. Crow didn't respond, electing to take another sip instead.

Richie looked at Aiden. "Do you know what time it is? I should give Kate a call."

Aiden raised his wristwatch to his face. "Mr. Brenadeir should be out any minute now."

"Oh, great. So, what time is it?"

Richie saw Aiden's attention drift away as his eyes slowly rose up to the loft.

"Speak of the devil," Aiden said, a smile stretching across his face.

Richie noticed countless faces tilting up in similar fashion, beaming with admiration. He shifted around and peered up to the loft. Looking down upon the flock was a white-haired man with a grey three-piece suit wrapped around spotted, artificially-tanned skin. His bright teeth shone in his smile like a neon light. He appeared to have aged well but still strived to appear younger—the kind of boomer who would jokingly challenge a person to an arm-wrestling contest but would be a little too serious about it. There was no doubt that this was William Brenadeir.

Mr. Brenadeir rested his hands on the wooden railing and smiled from ear to ear. "My peers, my colleagues, my friends, I'm so honored to have you all here. I truly feel blessed beyond words. We have an incredible night ahead of us. I notice some new faces in the crowd, and if this is your first time here, please know that whoever asked you to be here thinks extremely highly of you. You are in esteemed company.

"Allow me to introduce myself. I am William Lee Brenadeir. This estate was built by my great-grandfather, Arthur Lee Brenadeir. After several failures in the business world, he was given an opportunity by someone who saw greatness within him. He seized that opportunity and cultivated an extraordinary life. Later on in that quite extraordinary life, he believed it important to create opportunities for others, just as he was provided an opportunity. Tonight, opportunities will present themselves. Keep open eyes and an open mind, and you might just find yourself primed for greatness."

Brenadeir pressed his hands together and dipped his head to the crowd below. Applause erupted throughout the room as if the supposed networking event spontaneously transformed into a rock concert.

"Thank you, thank you," Brenadeir gave a giddy giggle. "I am truly grateful."

The applause died down to give Brenadeir the floor once again. "Of course, nights like these always start with a total lockdown to ensure privacy."

Mechanical gears groaned.

Richie whipped his head around to see metal climbing down the doors and windows.

"Don't worry," Brenadeir continued. "They're set to reopen in three hours via an automatic timer. I couldn't get them open even if I wanted to." He chuckled. "The automation is by design—again, for the purposes of privacy."

Richie's stomach dropped with the sudden realization that he was now trapped with complete strangers in a rich man's house, and every stranger was eyeballing him like a piece of meat.

Aiden gave him a quick look and smirked. He whispered, "It's all for show. The place isn't actually on lockdown."

Still, Richie remained skeptical as Brendaier continued.

"It is customary for first-time guests of the Brenadeir Manor to receive a tour. Mr. Melroy shall guide you to the first stop on the tour, where I will meet you soon. Please, have patience with me. My legs aren't what they used to be."

Mr. Brenadeir gave a soft chuckle before saying, "Oh, I feel so silly. I forgot to ask. Is everyone enjoying themselves?"

A thunderous eruption through the room rattled the floor beneath Richie. Either these people were the world's most egregious brown noses, or they genuinely idolized the man above them.

"Wonderful. So much enthusiasm, and the night is so young. First-time guests, I am eager to meet each of you in person. Please, follow Mr. Melroy, and I will see you soon."

Mr. Brenadeir waved and shuffled away from the railing to another round of feverish applause. Amidst that commotion, Richie tapped Aiden to get his attention.

"If I'm going on a tour of the place, I should check in with Kate first," Richie said.

"What's that?" Aiden leaned into Richie as the applause died down.

"I should really check in with Kate," Richie said a bit louder.

"Oh, yes, of course," Aiden replied.

The double doors at the front of the room slowly opened without assistance, and a sixty-five-year-old, tall, lean man with slicked-back grey hair and a tightly trimmed beard above a slim navy-blue suit strolled in, hands firmly clasped behind his back.

The man came to a firm stop and said, "Yes, I am Mr. Melroy. New guests, please follow me."

Mr. Melroy casually turned and walked back through the doors.

Aiden rested a hand on Richie's back and said, "You won't want to keep Mr. Brenadeir waiting. The tour won't take long."

Rubber-bottomed, discount shoes squeaked as the new guests walked towards the open doors. Tyler stopped when he realized Richie wasn't by his side.

"Hey, Big Rich," Tyler called back to Richie. "We stickin' together or what?"

Richie, apprehensive as all hell, looked at Aiden.

Aiden gave Richie a reassuring grin. "Buddy, I can see you're worried. But you have to understand ... you are in the presence of a man who has transformed countless lives. And you have the opportunity to speak with him directly. This is something people can't even dream of because they don't know it's within the realm of possibility. I can't in good conscience let you squander this chance when you have so much potential. I'll see to it that we get to your phone as soon as possible after your facetime with Mr. Brenadeir. I got your back. Have I steered you wrong yet?"

"Richie?" Tyler called to him again.

Richie let out an uneasy sigh, then gave Aiden a simple, "Okay."

"Atta boy," Aiden said with a grin. "I'm excited for you, my friend. I'll see you very soon."

Richie nodded to Aiden, trying to hide his discontent. Asking to check in with his pregnant partner wasn't asking much. But Richie was the only first-timer who had yet to proceed, and Tyler needed his new comrade.

7

R ichie caught up to Tyler, and they walked through the double doors together to join a group of six other first-timers following Mr. Melroy through a room lined with marble sculptures of nude gladiators.

"Hey, uh, Mr. Melroy," a pudgy redhead called out. "Is there any food on this tour? I need some grub."

Mr. Melroy continued to walk through the room without acknowledging the question.

"Damn," the redhead said to the tall, stone-faced guy with a buzz-cut walking next to him. "Mr. Melroy's cold as hell."

Stone Face didn't engage either, prompting the redhead to shout out loud enough for the group to hear, "Well, this is fun."

As the bunch continued to pass by grand gladiatorial statues, Richie scanned the company he was in. Each individual drastically differed in aesthetic from the well-to-do seasoned veterans of the event. Including Richie, the group was composed of six men and two women. The squatty redhead at the front of the group was the only man who wore a suit, but the wrinkled, cheap, mustard-colored fabric made it look more like a Halloween costume than a business suit. Stone Face, a head taller than the redhead, wore black jeans and a rugged brown coat. Behind them was Helena, who was easy to pick out based on Tyler's description: black dress, black combat boots, dark eyes accentuated by heavy eye makeup. The silent, mysterious Helena was the only person who didn't seem impressed by the surroundings, which led Richie to gather that she was either wealthy herself or simply didn't really care about anything in the unbearable "hipster" kind of way. Next to her was a woman in a black hoodie with bunned-up hair and a large scar from her temple to her lip, which Richie noticed as she glanced at the statues. Behind the two women were two men, one short and athletic with a button-up shirt and khakis hugging bulging quads, and one tall and muscled-up with a tight, black sweater on. Richie figured the tall one must've been Wade, the six-foot-four gym rat Tyler mentioned. Richie and Tyler brought up the rear.

Tyler leaned into Richie and quietly said, "Are we to assume that these statues of naked buff dudes are supposed to be that old bag of bones who owns the place?"

Richie muffled a laugh in his fist.

Mr. Melroy came to a wooden door with a carved cursive "B" stretching across it. He turned to the group and said, "This room holds a very special place in Mr. Brenadeir's heart. The artifacts you'll see are priceless and quite delicate. If you attempt to touch anything in the room, you will be promptly exiled. Understand?"

Each person in the group nodded, prompting Mr. Melroy to open the door and motion them in. "Welcome to the Brenadeir Game Chamber."

"Game Chamber?" Tyler whispered to Richie. "We playin' *Mortal Kombat* in this bitch?"

Richie mumbled, "Different kind of game."

It was more of a museum than a room. Glass cases held ancient spears, medieval weaponry, swords, suits of armor, antique handguns, and muskets. The walls were lined with old paintings of hunters and warriors through the ages, from Neanderthal to the American Revolutionary War, as well as old photos of big game hunters proudly posing next to large, dead animals.

"Jesus," Tyler whispered to Richie. "This family's really into killing things."

Mr. Melroy addressed the group, "Mr. Brenadeir will be down to greet you shortly. Feel free to look around and talk amongst yourselves."

Mr. Melroy shuffled out of the room and closed the door behind him.

"Oh," the redhead muttered. "Well, bye-bye, Mr. Melroy, I guess."

An awkward silence flowed through the group as they all studied each other.

"I'll start off the roll call." Tyler raised his hand as if he were being called on. "My name's Tyler and I'm *not* an alcoholic, but I *am* weirded the hell out."

The redhead chuckled. "My name's Mason. I work as a sales assistant at a marketing firm. 'Sales Assistant' is really just a generous title for 'he-who-does-bitch-work-for-assholes.' I was invited here by a sales guy in my office. He said I had potential. Not sure why he's being nice to me, but I'll take it."

"I'm Vince." The short man with the button-up shirt and khakis stepped forward. "I, uh ... I have a brain tumor. I was invited here to network with medical professionals who might be able to help."

"Damn," Stone Face said. "I'm sorry to hear that, brother."

"Thanks." Vince dropped his eyes. "It is what it is, ya know?"

"I'm Oliver," Stone Face said. "Got invited here by a guy who came into the hardware store I work at. Didn't have a good feeling about it, but ... I'm lookin' for a change, so I'll take a chance, I guess."

"Name's Wade." The tall, muscular man spoke with a low, deep voice. "I'm a bouncer. Was working the door at a pretty upscale club and some rich pricks told me to come here for a job opportunity. I figured some of these assholes need extra protection. Don't know why else I'd be here."

Richie took a step forward. "I'm Richie. I work in home renovation. Well, I *worked* in home renovation. Was working on a guy's house. We got to talking and he said I should come here."

Mason pointed to Richie's face and said, "Did he beat you up and force you here? Your eye's pretty busted."

Richie smirked. "Nah, I got into a dumb fight. Can't believe he still wanted to bring me here looking like this."

"Important question here," Helena's soft voice took the spotlight. "Anybody else getting big-time cult vibes? It can't just be me."

Mason looked over her black outfit and dark face makeup, and said, "You would probably know, am I right?"

Mason giggled to himself and looked around to see if anyone would join, but no one was amused.

Tyler interjected, "Not sure what ya mean, my guy."

Mason stopped laughing and went pale. "Oh, I mean ... Just because ... she's goth or emo or whatever."

"I'm a nonconformant anarchist who doesn't play well with others." Helena shot a daring look to Mason. "Nobody would want me in their cult."

"Well then," Mason smirked. "What do you do for work?"

"I work at a dog shelter," Helena said. "Because I'd rather spend my days with dogs than with humans."

"Heard that." Oliver nodded to her.

"Helena," Tyler said. "How did you get your invite?"

"My stepmother," Helena replied.

"Mrs. Vanderloo?" Tyler asked.

"Unfortunately, yes. She makes quite the impression. I don't like her at all, but ... my father died recently, and she begged me to spend some time with her. Not sure why I have to spend time with her in this place, but ..."

"Sorry for your loss," Vince said.

Helena nodded to him. "Thank you."

"Hey," Mason focused on the woman in the black hoodie, who was obviously avoiding attention. "We haven't heard from scarface yet."

She cocked her head and narrowed her eyes with a death stare. "What did you just call me?"

"Shit," Tyler said. "There's an asshole in every group, isn't there, Mason?"

"What?" Mason raised his hands in the air. "It's not a bad thing. I think the face scar's cool."

"Maybe I should call you the fat ginger," she shot back at him.

"Wow, everybody's so sensitive these days." Mason waved his hands in the air.

Wade stepped in and looked down at Mason. "Just shut up for a second."

Mason put his lips together and took a step back.

Wade looked over to the woman in the black hoodie. "What's your story?"

She finally took her eyes off Mason and said, "I'm Shelly. I work at a boxing gym. An older guy started training with me. He's a nice guy. A little too nice, honestly. I wish he would spend more time training and less time talking. But, I've told him a little bit about my past and ... he said I should come here and meet some people."

"Huh," Richie thought for a quick second. "So we have a boxer, a bouncer, a dog shelter worker, an assistant, a college dropout—Sorry, Tyler. No offense."

"None taken." Tyler shrugged.

Richie continued, "A hardware store clerk, a man with a tumor, and a guy who works with power tools. An interesting mix of people to mingle with the upper class."

"Holy shit." A lightbulb in Mason's head flickered wildly. "It's a Make-A-Wish situation. They're gonna give us money."

"I ain't a charity case," Shelly muttered. "If that's what this is, they can keep it."

Wade scoffed. "Hey, if some rich folks wanna give away their money, I wouldn't say 'no'. You guys know the easiest road to wealth in America? A fat trust fund at birth. I guarantee most of the people in this house right now were born with a handout. So they're the charity cases. It's just a different kind of charity."

"Hold on a sec," Oliver said as he scoped out the upper corners of the room. "They could be surveilling us."

Wade laughed. "You feeling the stranger danger there, big guy?"

Oliver continued to look around the room with distrust. "Just keeping my eyes open."

Out of the corner of his eye, Richie noticed Helena lower her head. He turned his attention to Helena and witnessed her wince and gently massage her temples. The rest of the group continued to deliberate as she stealthily wandered to the door.

Richie tapped Tyler. "Something's up with Helena."

Tyler shrugged. "What else is new? She's definitely got some big-time mental battle scars."

"I'm gonna go check on her," Richie said.

"Good man. Just be careful. I don't want to be judgmental, but ... she's a little spooky." Tyler patted Richie on the back.

Richie rolled his eyes at Tyler with a grin and walked over to Helena, who was holding herself up against the wall. He lifted his hand to tap her shoulder but stopped when he realized that she was whispering to herself, shaking her head left to right.

"What?" she whispered. "Stop, stop, slow down. I can't ... I can't understand ... Please, I can't ..."

"Um ..." Richie spoke softly. "Helena?"

Helena jerked her head and looked up at Richie with wide, blood-shot eyes. Her face was trembling with fear.

"Helena?" Richie took a small step back from her. "Are you ... okay?"

Helena's eyes darted left and right while her head remained still. "I ... I don't know."

"What's going on?"

Helena peered around the room. She settled herself and took a deep breath.

"I'm sorry if I freaked you out," Helena said. "I sometimes get this pulsing sensation in my head. It's like these little shocks. Just throws me off."

"It sounded like you were talking to someone," Richie said.

"Oh, um ... yeah, that's just how I calm myself down."

"Huh. You sure you're okay?'

Helena grunted in annoyance. "You're not a hero, dude. Calm down."

Helena trudged past him to join the group, leaving Richie behind.

"Okay, then," Richie uttered to himself. "That was weird."

At the far end of the room, the sounds of mechanical gears whirled through the walls, drawing the group's attention to wooden double doors. Richie walked back to Tyler's side.

Wade gave a sarcastic slow clap. "Come on, Mr. B. Better late than never. Sheesh."

Roaring motors halted and the wooden doors slowly slid open.

Mr. Brenadeir had arrived, shuffling out of the elevator with a massive smile. "Thank you for being so patient with me. I'm so grateful to meet you all." Mr. Brenadeir slowly grazed his sights over each of them.

Tyler spoke up. "Good evening, Mr. Brenadeir. Thank you for having us. This is all extremely impressive."

"Thank you for saying that, Mr. Tyler Grant."

"Oh ... You know my name, sir?" Tyler asked.

"Yes, of course." Mr. Brenadeir shuffled to a painting of a white-haired man in tan safari garb posing with a rifle. "My guests, the Brenadeirs have long been proud hunters. I guess you could say that hunting is in our blood. It might be strange, the thought of stuffy businessmen getting their hands dirty and preying on bigger, faster, stronger game. But, you see, it's vital that as you succeed in life, you remind yourself that you must fight to live. Nothing is guaranteed. And you must keep your teeth sharpened."

A silence filled the room as the group watched Mr. Brenadeir gaze at the painting with admiration.

Mr. Brenadeir finally turned his focus back to the group. "Each of you has been invited to the Brenadeir Estate because someone saw something remarkable in you. You have made a tremendous impression. This could be for a number of reasons: the obstacles you've overcome, the skills you possess, the potential you've shown. If you are here, it means that someone believes in you. If someone within my circle believes in you, then I believe in you. Now, each of you desires change, yes?"

Richie saw several heads begin to nod, and he joined in.

"It's admirable to strive for change, to strive for better," Mr. Brenadeir said. "Please, I would like to know what your greatest desires are."

Mr. Brenaider pointed to Mason. "Would you like to start, Mr. Mason Jones?"

"Okay." Mason puffed his chest out a bit in preparation to share. "I would love to be like you, sir. Work my way into being a top executive. I want to be a decision maker. Someone who's looked up to. Big house, beautiful wife, cars, boats. I want to have it all and want for nothing."

"Ah, big goals. Very big goals. And how about you, Mr. Vince Hines?"

Vince was a deer in headlights. "Oh, me? Sure, um ... Well, I guess my goals are a bit different at the moment. I would like to beat this tumor in my head. But the bigger issue is that my family isn't doing well. My father has an injury and can't work, and my mom's a teacher who's delivering pizzas at night to make ends meet. We're in quite a bit of debt, and cancer treatment is gonna put us in a huge hole. So whether I live or die, my goal, well ... my wish ... would be for them to be okay financially. I hate the thought that my illness, and ... my death ... could make things so much harder. There's nothing I wouldn't do for them."

"What a heart you have," Mr. Brenadeir said to Vince. "The heart of a warrior."

"Oh, um …" Mason jumped in. "Of course, my goals include giving much of my money to my parents. I'd like to buy them a house. They … gave birth to me, and cared for me … so …"

Tyler whispered to Richie, "Wow, nice save, Mason. We all think you're a great guy now."

Richie tried to quash his grin as best he could, then he caught Mr. Brenadeir looking directly at him. Richie cleared his throat and composed himself.

"Mr. Richie Stull," Mr. Brenadeir said. "What do you think of the aforementioned goals?"

"Oh … um," Richie stumbled through his words. "I'm sorry, but … I don't understand, sir."

"The goals of Mr. Mason Jones and Mr. Vince Hines? Do you believe one set of goals to be worth fighting for more than the other?"

Richie looked back and forth from Mason to Vince. "Oh, I … I'm not sure what to say."

"Please," Mr. Brenadeir said. "This is certainly a safe space. You are all free to speak your mind. I think it's an interesting discussion to have. We have Mr. Mason Jones, unhappy with his status as low man on the totem pole at his corporation. Perhaps he feels he's more skilled and more intelligent than many of the people who give him orders. He seems to desire being the one who gives the orders. With that power and responsibility comes financial success. And money makes the world go round, of course. Some say money can't buy happiness. Well, I can tell you that I am extremely happy, and wealth is a large contributing factor. So, Mr. Mason Jones would like wealth and power. Mr. Vince Hines is facing an incredible obstacle in his life. His family is in tremendous debt, and his treatment may put them in a hole they might not ever be able to crawl out of. They will have to rely on begging for help from friends, family, and strangers. Mr. Vince Hines' goals are to defeat cancer and to help his family avoid financial hardship. Mr. Richie Stull, do you believe one of these sets of goals to be worth fighting for more than another?"

"Um …" Richie took a moment to gather his thoughts. "I would have to say that Vince's goals are more selfless. So, I'd have to go with Vince."

"Ah, so you believe the goals of Mr. Vince Hines to be more noble, perhaps. But ... the question was ... which set of goals is more worth fighting for? What lengths would these two gentlemen go to in order to achieve their goals? Perhaps, the nobility of Mr. Vince Hines could be a hindrance in stepping on throats, so to speak, stabbing a back, so to speak, in order to achieve his goals."

Richie wasn't sure what to say. He was completely caught off guard by the interrogation.

Tyler took the pressure off of Richie. "It's a very interesting discussion to have, Mr. Brenadeir, sir. I certainly agree."

Mr. Brenadeir continued to await Richie's response as Richie felt himself shrinking with embarrassment.

"Yes," Mr. Brenadeir said. "It's a discussion not all of us are ready to have. Please, tell us about your goals, Mr. Tyler Grant."

Richie took a step forward to finally put his stamp on the conversation. "Sir ... I have a child on the way and just lost my job, both of which I'm sure you already know. I didn't just come from nothing; I came from less than that. I came from a black hole. I will work till my hands bleed on five minutes of sleep a night to make sure my child and the mother of my child have what they need. I would hope that I can do what I need to do without hurting others. Without stepping on throats and stabbing backs. I would hope that I can get ahead by being better than others, not worse."

A smile stretched across Mr. Brenadeir's face. He slowly lifted his hands, then clapped with vigor.

"Excellent!" Mr. Brenadeir shouted. "Simply excellent. I quite enjoyed that insight."

Tyler leaned in to Richie. "Dude, that was awesome."

"Mr. Tyler Grant," Mr. Brenadeir said. "What will you fight for?"

"To pay off my mom's medical debts and go back to college," Tyler said.

"Excellent. Mr. Wade Murrow?"

"Well," Wade started. "People don't think much of me. I guess I wanna just prove everybody wrong. To me ... yeah, that's worth fighting for."

"An excellent goal, I love it. Mr. Oliver Redding?"

Oliver tilted his neck, cracking it, while he thought of what to say. "Escape my past. Start fresh. Create a brand new life for myself."

"Wonderful. Ms. Helena Vanderloo?"

"Pass," Helena flippantly responded.

"Okay, I guess we'll come back to Ms. Helena Vanderloo. How about you, Ms. Shelly Pavia?"

Shelly's hands were firmly in the hand warmer of her hoodie, clearly trying to avoid attention. "I just do what I gotta do. Just survive. Any means necessary."

"Ah, yes." Mr. Brenadeir pointed at Shelly and winked. "It's very early, but from what I've heard, you might just be my favorite, Ms. Shelly Pavia."

"I'm sorry," Tyler raised his hand. "But, favorite for what exactly?"

Mr. Brenadeir's eyes illuminate with excitement. "My favorite to grab a life-changing opportunity by the horns. Can't you feel it in the air? Can't you practically taste it?"

"And, um," Mason raised his hand. "What exactly is that opportunity?"

"Oh, in due time, ladies and gentlemen," Mr. Brenadeir said. "In due time."

Mr. Brenadeir checked his wristwatch. "Oh my. Where does the time go? We must continue the tour. I invite you all to board the elevator."

Mr. Brenadeir opened a hand out to the elevator not far behind him. The group looked around at each other.

Mason shrugged. "Yeah, what the hell? Let's see more of this castle."

Richie whispered to Tyler as they walked in the back of the group, "Are we ever gonna get to go home?"

"Seeing how this guy moves," Tyler said. "Wouldn't count on being in bed any time soon."

"A certain pregnant somebody is gonna be pissed."

"If you leave here with an apprenticeship and on your way to six figures before you hit twenty-five, I think she'll be a little forgiving."

Richie sighed with discontent.

"Hey," Tyler said. "If he tries anything funny, I think we can take him."

Tyler lifted his knuckles to Richie for a fist bump. Richie chortled and went knuckle to knuckle with him.

The group passed by Mr. Brenadeir one by one as they entered the open elevator. Richie was the last to file in. He turned around to see Mr. Brenadeir smiling from outside the elevator.

"What a group we have here." Mr. Brenadeir placed his hand over his heart. "I'll see you soon."

Mr. Brenadeir pressed the button outside the elevator doors, and a gate quickly slid shut in front of Richie's face.

"Woah, wait," Richie said. "You're not coming?"

"Oh, it's far too crowded in there. I'll be on the next one."

"Oh," Richie looked around the elevator to see that everyone was just as perplexed that the leader of the tour would take a different route. "Okay?"

The doors began to slide over the gate.

"Good luck, my new friends." Mr. Brenadeir waved to them as he disappeared behind the sliding elevator doors.

The tin box that Richie and the others were huddled together in was draped in silence. It stayed that way for long enough to kindle confusion. The lights dimmed around them until they were almost completely in darkness. Silence gave way to quickened breaths and heartbeats.

Tyler said what everyone was thinking: "Why aren't we moving?"

Why had Mr. Brenadeir wished them good luck? Richie's stomach churned at the thought that the night might have gone from weird to bad. He heard a faint groan from Helena and turned to her to see her wincing, just as she had before. She grabbed chunks of her hair.

"Something's wrong," Helena muttered through her dishevelled mane.

"What is it?" Richie's dry throat barely got the question out.

"Helena?" Tyler put a hand on her back.

Helena whispered, "We're not alone in here."

Mason gulped. "What did she just say?"

Lights flashed on and blanketed them in red. The elevator rumbled under their feet, and they began a slow descent with a *BEEP ... BEEP ... BEEP*.

Tyler leaned in to Helena, "We're not alone? What are you saying?"

Helena whimpered, "Something's really, really wrong."

Wade shouted at Helena, "What's wrong?! What are you talking about?!"

Richie jammed the buttons beside the door. "Why are we still going down?"

Tyler stepped up beside Richie and jammed the buttons with him. "We were on the first floor. How many floors could be under us?"

The elevator's descent quickened, and the beeps became more frequent. They were dropping stories and stories at a rapid rate.

"Oh, God!" Oliver uttered. "Oh, my lord in heaven. I'm so sorry for straying, Lord! Don't let this be it! Don't let this be it!"

Helena mumbled to herself and slapped her head. "Too many! Too many voices!"

Mason sank into the nearest corner. "The crazy girl's going crazy!

Tyler shot his wide, quivering eyes at Richie. "What the hell are they doing with us?"

Richie felt his heart in his throat. The panicked screams and groans blended with the buzzing of the hyperactive mechanisms controlling their fate.

8

They met when they were too young to realize the feelings they gave each other. Richie just knew that he was drawn to Kate in a way that made him happier than he thought he was worthy of feeling. For nearly a decade, she was his first thought when he awoke, his last thought before he fell asleep, and the most common element of his dreams. She was the only thing on his mind as the roaring red elevator plummeted to unknown depths.

Finally ... Richie felt the elevator begin to slow in its descent.

Through wild breaths, Mason shouted, "We're–we're slowing down! Are we slowing down?"

The elevator whimpered as it slowed to a stop. Panicked breaths of the sweat-stained group ricocheted off the walls. Richie and Tyler slowly stepped away from the elevator door.

Tyler uttered, "Who's gonna be on the other side of that door?

Wade held his clenched fist in front of his chin. "Whoever they are, they don't wanna see me right now."

Helena fell to her knees, palming her scalp. "Stop yelling at me!"

Mason yelled to Helena, "Who are you talking to?!"

"The voices!" Helena shouted.

"What are they saying?!" Oliver cried out.

"They're saying ..." Helena gritted her teeth and squinted her eyes in agony. "They're saying ..."

Helena's eyes shot open, and the blood drained from her face. "Oh, no."

DING.

The elevator door slowly crept open, and the group scattered to either wall, ramming into each other as they ducked, except for Wade, who stood tall and defiant in full view of the open door. From his crouching position, Richie peered up at Wade standing with his fists at the ready.

"What do you see?" Richie whispered.

"Can't see anything," Wade said. "Just a dark room."

Light flashed on and illuminated Wade, who held a hand to his eyes to shield them. He lowered his hand and cocked his head in confusion.

"What the hell?" Wade muttered under his breath.

Richie peeked his head out to the opening to see a small, grungy, grey room with rusty benches and lockers. The floor tiles wrapped around a black crest in the shape of a shield in the center of the floor, ten feet by four feet, with the familiar cursive letter B across it. The moldy tile floor was caked in large crimson stains, most of which were in front of the steel double doors on the wall opposite the elevator.

"It looks like a ..." Richie thought for a moment. "A locker room."

"Who's out there?" Mason's voice trembled.

"There's no one." Richie slowly rose to his feet. "It's empty."

Tyler poked his head out. "I don't understand."

Wade stayed on guard as he inched out of the elevator.

"Hey, man," Mason shook his head at Wade. "Don't go out there."

"And stay on the elevator to hell?" Wade shot back.

Richie followed Wade out of the elevator, his eyes darting in every direction. Tyler stayed on Richie's hip, holding his shaky fists up, like Wade, but with much less self-assuredness. Shelly's jaws bouldered out as she took a few steps outside the elevator and scoped the room out like she was ready for war. Vince saw the bravery exuding from Shelly and hunched behind her.

Shelly felt Vince on her back, and without looking, she said, "What are you doin'?"

"I, uh ..." Vince stuttered. "I got your six."

Shelly scoffed. "No, you don't."

In the elevator, Oliver crouched down and tapped Helena. "Who were the voices?"

Helena glanced at Oliver's eyes, then quickly looked away. "I don't know."

"Was it the devil?" Oliver asked.

Helena met Oliver's eyes, and her nostrils flared as her breathing quickened.

"Was it?" Oliver asked again.

Helena moved her parched lips to Oliver's ear, and whispered, "There are worse things."

Oliver backed his face away from Helena and saw an intense fear in her quivering eyes. Helena staggered to her feet and stumbled out of the elevator. Oliver rose up, his eyes wide with worry.

"No, no, no!" Mason remained crouched in a corner of the elevator. "Take me back up! Take me back up!"

BEEP.

"*Hello,*" A calm, uncannily soothing feminine voice sounded from speakers above the lockers. "*All contestants must exit the elevator.*"

"Contestants?" Richie mumbled to himself.

"*Failure to exit the elevator will result in elimination.*"

"What?" Tyler said. "What the hell is 'elimination'?"

Helena wrapped her arms around her stomach and vomited on her boots. She wiped her mouth and mumbled, "Death."

"What did you say?" Richie zeroed in on Helena.

Helena's weak knees forced her to hold herself up against a locker. "Elimination. I ... I think it means death."

Richie looked over to the elevator. Oliver was frozen in fear, unable to move as Mason whimpered, curled up in a ball beside him.

"*Elimination in ... Ten ... Nine ...*"

"We gotta get them out!" Richie rushed to the elevator, and Tyler followed as the countdown continued.

Richie slapped Oliver's cheek. "Snap out of it, man! You gotta move!"

"*Six ... Five ...*"

Richie grabbed Oliver's arm and yanked him out of the elevator. He looked back at Tyler struggling to subdue a flailing, howling Mason.

"*Three ...*"

Richie plunged back into the elevator just as Shelly rushed in. They joined Tyler in grabbing a handful of Mason's jacket and dragged him clear of the elevator door, just as—

SHINK!

The elevator door slid shut in a blink. Richie, Tyler, and Shelly fell to the floor, catching their breath.

Richie looked over at Tyler. "You okay?"

Tyler nodded to him with his chest jumping out of control.

Shelly jumped up and towered over Mason. "That's the last time I help you! Get your shit together!"

Mason wiped tears from his eyes as he attempted to gather himself. Richie got up and helped Tyler to his feet.

"*8 contestants remain.*"

"What's this contestants shit?!" Wade shouted to the ceiling. "I'm not playing anybody's game! You hear me?! Somebody better do some talkin'!"

The speakers crackled as a condescending "*ahem*" came through.

"*Hello, guests.*" It was unmistakably Mr. Brenadeir's voice.

"Brenadeir, you wrinkly old bastard!" Wade bellowed. "What the hell's goin' on here?!"

"*Yes, I understand this must be quite puzzling. I promised a night full of incredible opportunities. Now, your opportunity finally presents itself. You all have been selected to compete in a series of games that will test you as you've never been tested before. You will be pushed beyond your limits and, hopefully, come to find that you are capable of more than you ever thought possible.*"

"You're serious?!" Tyler called out.

"*This is very serious. And exciting.*"

"You're forcing us to play games for … what?!" Vince shouted. "Your entertainment?!"

"*Oh, well, while entertainment is certainly an undeniable aspect, we enjoy providing opportunities to people in need.*"

"What?!" Tyler shouted. "This is your twisted version of altruism? Forcing house guests to do things against their will?

"*No, no, we are not forcing you all to do anything. Participation is a choice.*"

"You expect us to believe that?" Richie growled.

Mason whimpered. "No, no, no. This can't be happening. This can't be happening."

"Why us?" Oliver queried. "Why were we chosen?"

"*Each of you has much to fight for. Some of you have children, signif-icant others, family members, or other acquaintances who are counting on you. That may differ from person to person. What unites you all is despair. Each of you has a significant amount of debt to your name or to your family's name. Medical debts, gambling debts, student loans, credit cards, family debts. All of you are looking for a way to break free from a lower-class life while desperately attempting to chip away at debt that accumulates faster than can be quelled. Some of you are staring down the barrel of death by a sheer twist of fate or have suicidal ideations brought on by the persistent overwhelming burdens you face. Tonight, we will see how much life truly means to you. What's more, tonight, you will be granted the opportunity to change your life forever."*

"You rich prick. You're sick," Shelly said through clenched teeth.

"I'm sorry you feel that way, Ms. Shelly Pavia. Many have taken advantage of this opportunity and have gone on to become incredible contributors to society. Executives, job creators, politicians, true titans of industry and influence. I implore you to reconsider."

Wade's fists began to loosen up. "And what exactly do we win?"

"Before we reveal the prize, let's introduce the contestants to the audience, shall we?"

Uproarious applause erupted from beyond the steel double doors. Richie felt the ground tremble under his boots.

CREEEEEAK.

The rusted doors parted methodically, causing the applause to grow incrementally louder until cheers and whistles reverberated through the locker room. Richie could only see darkness on the other side of the door, but the crowd sounded stadium-sized.

The speakers crackled, and a soothing, feminine voice sounded. *"All contestants must exit or face elimination."*

Mason smacked his cheek repeatedly. "Wake up! Wake up!"

Richie looked over to Tyler, who was shaking his head in disbelief.

"What do we do?" Tyler whispered.

"I don't think we have a choice," Richie said.

Tyler grabbed Richie's shirt and pulled him in. "Whatever happens, we stick together. Okay? Don't leave me alone."

Richie put a clammy hand on Tyler. "We stick together. You and me. We'll figure this out."

"Not sure if friendship's gonna work for these twisted assholes," Wade said. "Screw it. My life can't get worse anyways."

Wade puffed out his chest and trudged out of the room. Cheers immediately exploded like a celebrity musician revealing themselves on stage.

"They were never gonna help me just for the sake of helping me," Vince said. "I'm a dead man walking. Desperate. Hopeless. Just a sideshow."

Vince hung his head as he shuffled to the open doors. More applause darted through the air. Shelly followed with a scowl of defiance.

A *CLUCK-CLUCK-CLUCK* sound drew Richie's attention to Oliver, who was nervously clicking his tongue in his open mouth, drenched in sweat. Oliver suddenly snapped himself free of his daze and shot his eyes over to Helena, who was slumped on a bench with her head in her hands. Oliver rushed to her and took a knee to meet her face.

"What are they saying? What are the voices saying?" Oliver asked.

"Nothing. I can't hear them anymore," Helena answered with closed eyes.

"Where are they?" Oliver tapped her hand.

"They were found ... and punished." Helena whimpered.

Oliver swallowed the tiny bead of saliva he had left in his desert-dry throat.

The voice announced, "*All contestants must exit or face permanent forfeiture.*"

Richie and Tyler's eyes met, and Richie said, "You ready?"

Tyler took a few fluttering breaths before replying, "Ready for what?"

Richie looked down at the blood stains reaching towards the open doors in front of him and Tyler. Richie took the first step, and Tyler moved with him, nearly glued to Richie's hip. As Richie neared the black void beyond the door frame, the chatter from the crowd amplified. When Richie edged through the opening, a blast of belligerent adoration pounded the air around him like a physical object attacking him with flailing blows. Richie gazed up at rows upon rows of boisterous men in suits, with small sprinkles of women in dresses. The rows circled around a spotlit floor of sand surrounded by stone walls.

An underground coliseum.

Richie saw Wade, Vince, and Shelly in the middle of the sand floor, gazing up at the crowd. He inched forward little by little with Tyler at his back. Another thunder of applause flew through the bunker as Oliver, Helena, and Mason meandered out of the locker room like lost puppies. Richie stood at Shelly's side and could barely make out anything through the flaring spotlight shining down on them.

"We're dead." Mason crumpled beside Tyler's feet. "We're so dead, man!"

"Ladies and gentlemen!" Mr. Brenadeir's voice echoed.

A spotlight burst onto the first row where Mr. Brenadeir was peacocking in front of a microphone stand.

"Thank you all for being here for yet another edition of Night Games!"

The crowd erupted with applause. Richie looked through the faces of the people staring down at them, until he finally saw Aiden, who had the shittiest of shit-eating grins on his face. Aiden noticed Richie's gaze and gave Richie an enthusiastic thumbs up.

"Let's get to know our contestants," Mr. Brenadeir said as the overhead light narrowed to illuminate only Wade. "Mr. Wade Murrow. Twenty-four years of age. A career social club security doorman who constantly flirts with homelessness and death due to narcotic drug use. A once promising athlete, his athletic aspirations were derailed by injury, anger issues, legal troubles, and narcissism. His parents cut ties with him after he hospitalized his uncle in a drunken rage. Mr. Wade Murrow is playing for a clean record, redemption, a total reduction of debt, and wealth beyond his wildest dreams."

The spotlight moved to Vince.

"Mr. Vince Hines. Twenty-five years of age. A high-IQ individual with a loving family who believed he had a bright future ahead, before learning that a brain tumor was threatening to cut his life short. Life can be unfair and merciless. But with wealth and power, anything is possible. Mr. Vince Hines is playing for the best treatment money can buy, a total reduction of debt, and wealth beyond his wildest dreams. Moving on ..."

The deafening roars never ceased as Mr. Brenadeir introduced the people below. Richie's eyes darted in every direction searching for a way out, but to no avail. He was an animal in a cage being gawked at.

"Ms. Shelly Pavia. Twenty-four years of age. A youth boxing champion with numerous run-ins with the law, she has found it difficult to move ahead in life with the public suspicion that she murdered her parents at age eighteen looming over her head, though she was exonerated. After giving birth to a child whose father disappeared from the picture, Ms. Shelly Pavia is playing for a clean record, a blessed life for her child, a total reduction of debt, and wealth beyond her wildest dreams."

"Mr. Mason Jones. Twenty-five years of age. A young man who inherited his father's crippling gambling addiction, which has been amplified by the innovation of personal computers and the internet. Nearing a very impressive five hundred thousand dollars in gambling debts at such a young age, Mr. Mason Jones is likely to be heading to prison, which will leave his brother without a caregiver, as their parents died while his mother was driving under the influence. Mr. Mason Jones will be playing for a full-time, life-long caregiver for his brother, a total reduction of debt, and wealth beyond his wildest dreams."

"How do they know this?!" Mason shrieked. "How could they know all this?!"

Mr. Brenadeir continued. "Mr. Oliver Redding. Twenty-two years of age. After leaving the radical militant cult he was raised in, he is under constant threat of violence from cult members unhappy with his decision to leave. He has recently fallen in love and fears violence will soon be directed towards them. He will be playing for a new identity, a guaranteed separation from said cult, and wealth beyond his wildest dreams."

"Mr. Tyler Grant. Twenty-one years of age. He recently dropped out of college to earn money for his mother's cancer treatment. He is risking his future while fighting a financial battle that he and his family have already lost. He will be playing for the world's best cancer treatment for his mother, a total reduction of debt, and wealth beyond his wildest dreams."

"Mr. Richie Stull. Twenty-three years of age. The product of a troubled past that saw him in and out of juvenile detention. He recently lost his job just hours after receiving news from his girlfriend that he has a baby on the way. Together, they have a mountain of debt without a support system to help. He will be playing for a total reduction of debt and wealth beyond his wildest dreams."

Amidst wild cheers, Richie once again laid eyes on Aiden, who was clapping like a maniac and pointing at himself. He was making a show of his accomplishment in bringing in such a fine contestant. Under the bright light, Richie felt his skin crawl and his stomach turn.

"And finally, Ms. Helena Vanderloo," Mr. Brenadeir said as the spotlight shifted to Helena. "Twenty-three years of age. A very precarious entry from the ever-eccentric Mrs. Darlene Vanderloo, widow of the deceased Mr. Thomas Vanderloo. Ms. Helena Vanderloo is riddled with grief after her father's suicide. She suspects foul play in her father's death, and she has gone so far as attempting to contact the dead for answers. She will be playing for all of the resources for a thorough investigation into the circumstances surrounding her father's death and wealth beyond her wildest dreams."

The spotlight widened until all eight were lit.

"Ladies and gentlemen," Mr. Brendadeir said with exaggerated bravado. "These are your contestants. Of the eight, the contestant to receive the most black cards should come as no surprise: Mr. Wade Murrow. Mr. Wade Murrow is followed by Mr. Oliver Redding, Mr. Vince Hines, and Mr. Richie Stull. The lowest black card recipients are Ms. Shelly Pavia, Mr. Tyler Grant, Mr. Mason Jones, and our fiercest underdog of the night, Ms. Helena Vanderloo. Place your bets accordingly. Contestants, you will be boldly competing in a series of battles with no rules and only one goal: win and advance. People of the Red Night, are ... you ... READY?!"

The walls shook as the crowd went insane with aggressive joy. Richie looked at the people standing next to him and saw that they were just as terrified.

"Hey, asshole!" Wade shouted up at Mr. Brenaider amidst the chaotic applause.

Wade's words were swallowed by the rampant noise of the onlookers, but Mr. Brenadeir noticed Wade wave to get his attention.

Mr. Brenadeir said into the microphone, "Hold on a second, folks."

A raised hand from Mr. Brenadeir was enough for the crowd's collective volume to silence.

"One of our contestants would like to say something," Mr. Brenadeir continued. "Mr. Wade Murrow, please speak loudly."

"What happens if we lose?" Wade shouted up.

"Well, Mr. Wade Murrow," Mr. Brenadeir said. "Have you not already lost? We are offering you a brand-new life. You will be able to earn money each round, all leading to the aforementioned earnings package. Each earnings package has been tailored to each of your individual needs. In addition, if you win, you earn a seat at our grand society, the People of the Red Night!"

Mr. Brenadeir opened his arms wide to elicit a barrage of cheers.

"Cut the shit!" Spit flung from Richie's mouth as he shouted up at Mr. Brenadeir.

"Oh, another question?" Mr. Brenadeir motioned for the crowd to quiet down.

"If we lose," Richie said. "Do we die?"

"Oh, my," Mr. Brenadeir said into the microphone. "I'm sorry if you've gotten the impression that we would be entertained by death. No, we are entertained by the competition. You all are our featured guests. Once an elimination has occurred, the eliminated contestant shall leave with all of the wealth they have earned from this opportunity. Death shall not befall any of you."

Richie didn't find the statement convincing, but he had no choice but to accept it.

"Contestants, remember what you are playing for ... and who you are playing for," Mr. Brenadeir bellowed. "Without further ado, let the Night Games begin!"

With the ovation of the crowd, the light shining down on the group turned from white to red.

9

U nder the red glow and the roar of the crowd, Richie stood atop the sand feeling smaller than he'd ever felt before.

"Y'all think they're serious?" Wade said, looking up at the crowd with clenched fists. "They'll give us everything they said they would? Or are they just fuckin' with us for fun?"

Mason waddled on his shaky legs. "Wake up, man! They have all the money in the world and an underground fighting ring, I think they could do literally anything they wanted to!"

Wade pointed a finger at Mason. "You're starting to annoy the hell outta me. If we're dying, I'll make sure you die first!"

"Woah, woah," Vince stood between Wade and Mason. "We can't turn on each other."

"Were you not listening? That's exactly what we're supposed to do!" Wade clapped back.

The grains began to shake beneath Richie's feet. He turned and backed away from the trembling sand, as did the rest of the group. Between the group, the sand disappeared in a crevice as mechanical gears whirled, until a circular hole formed in the middle of the floor. More mechanical shifting blared from the hole as a round, steel platform arose. Richie and the others stood around the platform, sand continuing to roll off the edges, and saw thick tree branches and stones of different shapes and sizes lying scattered on the platform. At the north end of the arena, a stone pillar rose from the sand, settling three feet high. Then a south pillar, then east, then west.

Richie murmured to himself, "What the hell are those for?"

Richie heard a faint thud on the sand and turned to see Helena lying completely motionless.

"Helena?!" Oliver rushed to her side and put his ear to her lips.

Richie shouted out, "Is she breathing?"

"Yeah, thank God," Oliver replied.

Mr. Brenadeir shouted, "Round one: Sticks and stones. Contestants will have three minutes to stand atop one of the four pillars. At the end of three minutes, the four contestants standing atop the pillars will earn one hundred dollars and an advantage in the next round. Keep in mind that with each round the prize money rises significantly. While the starting prize may seem low, we must first witness your determination to see what potentially lies beyond the first step. Success comes to those willing to strive for more than what is initially offered. Contestants may use the provided weapons to complete their objective."

Richie looked up to the crowd and waved his hands wildly. "Wait! We need medical attention down here!"

No onlookers seemed to care that Helena had fallen.

The calming feminine voice sounded out through the coliseum. *"Round one: Sticks and stones. Potential earnings: One hundred dollars."*

Richie turned back to the group, each individual in a state of confusion.

"Three minutes starts ... now."

Under the raucous crowd, the contestants, minus the downed Helena, stood around the steel platform looking around at each other, checking who would be the first to make a move. Richie noticed Mason getting extra twitchy.

"So ..." Richie mumbled.

Mason lunged to the platform, clutched a jagged stone the size of his palm, and backed away from the group with paranoia beaming from his eyes. He looked over at the person closest to him: Shelly. She swiped a thick branch and wielded it like a baseball bat.

"Don't you look at me like that," Shelly growled at Mason.

"I know you guys are gonna team up on me!" Mason held the stone at ear level. "You think I'm weak!"

"Hey, now," Richie chimed in. "We can figure this out. We have to keep our heads."

"What's to figure out?" Wade asked as he walked to the pillar nearest him. "The game is simple." He leapt up onto the pillar and shouted, "Stand up on one of these after three minutes! Well, probably about two-thirty now! With what they're offering, you couldn't peel me off of this rock!"

Mason hurled the stone at Shelly, hitting her in the forehead, and sprinted away towards a pillar.

"Bitch!" Shelly exclaimed, holding her bleeding head. She darted after Mason, who was mounting the pillar, grabbed one of his legs, and yanked him onto the ground. Vince grabbed a branch off the platform and beelined for an open pillar as Shelly sent her boot into Mason's gut. Blood drained from Shelly's head to Mason's jacket.

"Stay down!" Shelly shouted at Mason.

"*Two minutes remaining.*"

"Oh, God!" Oliver shouted as he lifted Helena's back off the ground and brought her face to his. "Helena, ask the voices what happens next! Helena, wake up!"

Helena remained pale and limp.

"Christ." Oliver dropped Helena like a potato sack.

Oliver sprinted for the last open pillar. Tyler left Richie's side to cut Oliver off.

"Wait, wait!" Tyler pleaded. "You're bigger and stronger than me. Whatever we do next, I need an advantage more than you do."

Oliver shoved Tyler aside, sending Tyler tripping over his own feet and flailing into the platform head first with a thud.

"Hey!" Richie bellowed at Oliver while racing to Tyler's aid.

Wade clapped for Oliver. "There ya go, big guy! I was worried you didn't have it in you!"

Oliver hung his head as he mounted the pillar.

"*One minute remaining.*"

"What are we gonna do, Richie?" Tyler groaned as Richie helped him to his feet.

"Hey, Rich!" Wade shouted. "That kid's gonna get you killed!"

"Shut up!" Richie screamed at Wade.

"Get off me!" The shriek from Shelly caught Richie's attention.

Mason had pulled Shelly off the pillar and was beating her over the back with a thick branch. Richie bolted around the platform and tackled Mason to the ground.

"What are you doing?!" Mason shouted. "Don't help her!"

Richie shifted over to Shelly and said, "Are you okay?"

Shelly wheezed and shoved Richie's hand away.

"Please, let me up!" Richie heard Tyler plead to Vince from below the pillar Vince was standing on.

"I'm sorry. I have to win," Vince said as he kicked at Tyler's hands.

A desperate gasp for oxygen zipped through the sky from the open mouth of Helena, suddenly fully conscious. Her bones crackled as she shifted onto all fours, as if she wasn't in control of her own body. After a few deep breaths, a black, viscous liquid spewed from her mouth.

Richie rushed to her. "Helena, are you okay?"

"I think I know how to beat the games," Helena whispered in his ear.

"What?" Richie moved in closer.

"The winners of this round will choose who they fight next. You have to choose me."

"What? I don't know what you're saying."

A low, guttural growl came from Helena's mouth. She rapidly turned her head to Richie, revealing that her eyes had been replaced by swirling black holes.

"Win this round! And choose her!" Helena barked at Richie with an otherworldly voice.

Richie jumped backward in fright and crawled away from Helena just as she collapsed to the sand.

"*Thirty seconds.*"

"Richie! Help!" Tyler called out.

"I'm sorry!" Vince cried. "My family needs me! I need the advantage!"

Richie looked up to see Vince on top of Tyler pummeling him with his fists. Richie took off, grabbed a girthy branch from the platform, and cracked it across Vince's back. Vince rolled on the ground like a rag doll.

Tyler wiped blood from his mouth as he said, "Richie, I need to get on one of those rocks."

"Go ahead," Richie said.

"What about you?"

"I'll be fine. Go." Richie shoved Tyler towards the open pillar.

"Fifteen seconds."

Richie looked around him. Oliver, Wade, and Shelly were on a pillar, with Tyler mounting the fourth. Mason was down, Helena was unconscious, and Vince had just gotten on his feet, deliriously zig-zagging.

"I hope all the games are as easy as this!" Wade hollered with a grin taking up half his face.

"Hey, my guy with the brain tumor!" Wade yelled to Vince. "I'm just gonna say what everybody's thinkin' ... You don't have that long to live anyway, right? Why don't you just bow out and save us all the energy?!"

"*Ten ...*"

Vince steadied himself as he glared at Wade. Vince clenched his fists and gritted his teeth.

"*Eight ...*"

Vince charged toward Wade and let out a shrieking roar. Wade's smile faded as Vince gained on him.

"*Six ...*"

Richie saw a potential opening and he took it. He sprinted behind Vince, following him as he gunned for Wade.

"*Four ...*"

Vince catapulted from the ground and buried a shoulder into Wade's ankles, swiping Wade's feet from under him and sending him airborne. Vince crashed onto the sand behind the pillar, Wade smacking his jaw onto the pillar and bouncing onto the ground beside Vince in a daze. Richie leapt onto the pillar just as he heard—

"*Two.*"

Richie stood atop the pillar and turned to see Tyler scurry atop the final pillar.

BEEP.

"*Round complete.*"

Ecstatic applause wrapped around Richie like the world's worst hug. The crowd roared for the victors atop the pillars: Richie, Oliver, Tyler, and Shelly.

"Congratulations, contestants!" Mr. Brenadeir yelled into the microphone. "What a nailbiter! You four have earned one hundred dollars and an advantage in the next round!"

"Son of a bitch!" Wade wiped blood from his forehead and looked at Vince. "You're dead!"

Wade got to his feet and trudged to Vince, who was still down.

"No, no, no, Mr. Wade Murrow," Mr. Brendair said. "The round is over and physical engagement between rounds is considered cheating."

"I don't care!" Wade yelled, clenching his fists as he hovered over Vince.

"You would be forfeiting, Mr. Wade Murrow. You would no longer be granted this opportunity."

Vince held his palms above his face, preparing for a blow as Wade glared down at him. Wade loosened his hands and spit at his feet. He quickly turned and trotted away.

Wade muttered, "Like these assholes got where they are by following the damn rules."

The four pillars slowly lowered until all eight contestants were back on the sand. The platform returned to the ground and was covered by sliding steel doors. Richie bolted for Helena and shook her shoulders. Tyler, Oliver, and Vince followed suit.

"You still with us?" Richie said.

Helena's eyes opened, and she screamed out in terror, crawling backward away from everyone.

"What? What is it?" Richie took a few steps towards her while the others backed away.

"She's off her meds, that's what happened," Wade snarked.

"Now for a brief intermission," Mr. Brenadeir said. "Contestants: You may retreat to the waiting room."

10

When the elevator doors in the waiting room opened, Aiden Prince was on the other side.

Aiden shot the group a cheesy smile. What a difference an hour made on Richie's image of Aiden Prince. The snake oil salesman meets Silicon Valley tech bro was still visible, exuding that confident energy that only those in the same wealth bracket could feed off of, but now that smile contained something sinister. Features of his face were a bit more crooked, the skin a bit tighter. The smile would welcome the demise of someone like the idle contestants.

Richie was looking at a demon in a seven-thousand-dollar suit.

Aiden clapped his hands once as he walked to the middle of the room. "Great show, everyone. Great show."

Richie stared up at him, through him, into him, his jaw taught like a tightrope. Aiden's expression didn't falter as he caught the look. Unwavering swagger and positivity.

"Richie, could I have a moment of your time, please?" Aiden asked.

With nothing else to do but wait, Richie stood.

"Don't worry, everyone," Aiden continued. "I'll bring him back soon. Should they choose to touch base, your sponsors will be with you shortly." He raised his hand toward the elevator, and Richie walked toward it.

They spent a few silent moments in lockstep, side-by-side, then waited for the elevator doors to open. Richie's mind was in knots, tangled together in an unintelligible mess of tangents, questions, accusations, expressions of anger.

Once the elevator doors were closed, it was Aiden who spoke first. "You did well out there, Richie. I would say I'm proud of you, but I expected a lot of fight. Instead, I'll say I'm very pleased with what you did."

"Where are you taking me?"

"*Taking* you?" Aiden chuckled again as the elevator slowed its ascent. "I understand how your trust in me has been eroded. Relax. I'm just giving you a tour of the mansion. The parts you haven't seen yet."

The elevator doors opened to a corridor on the fourth floor, a space wider than the trailer Richie grew up in as a kid, with a gaudy purple carpet and green doors lining the walls.

Aiden stepped out, but Richie didn't follow.

"Were you spying on me in the bar?" Richie asked.

Aiden turned back to Richie, and the look on his face was the answer Richie expected.

Richie clenched his jaw. "You saw that I could handle myself in a bar room scrap and brought me out here to fight people like me ... for the pleasure of people like you."

The doors of the elevator began to close. Aiden put his hand up, halting the doors' progress. "Mr. Brenadeir creates opportunities for people in need. Whatever your perspective is, the sooner you change it the better. You want to pretend like you don't know how the world works? Go ahead. You want to go back to being a day laborer begging for a site manager position and more quote-unquote *responsibility*? You wanna run your own home maintenance business? Fine by me. What happens when the economy tanks and no one's looking to get an extension on their home? Where do you fit within that race to the bottom, begging for a project with the promise that you can come in at the lowest price? What happens when another round of inflation causes the cost of raw materials to increase even higher than it is now and you have to cut into your margins to get your gigs? You think painting apartments is going to help keep you afloat when the money-maker projects get stuck in limbo?"

Aiden took a moment to catch his breath. His face softened. He straightened up, his hand still fixed on the elevator door. "You and everyone inhabiting this godforsaken planet are at the whims of systems. You know the difference between people like you and people like me? I'll give you a hint, it's not that I'm smarter than you. Intellectually, I can assume with absolute certainty that you'd run circles around me. The difference is that I say fuck the systems in place and you try to squeeze whatever sloppy bullshit you can get from those dried up little teets you call employment, government, what have you. The difference between a millionaire and the other 99% is that we don't *earn* ... We *take*. You will never become prosperous unless someone shows you the path. You might be comfortable at some point, but even then, you'll have a mountain of debt just waiting to fall on you, your girlfriend, your child-to-be. And that's because you *earn* and don't *take*.

"You have a chance now to be a taker. And you can be as angry as you want that you're fighting for the enjoyment of some snot-nosed elites that would spit on you in public if they weren't afraid of backlash to their public image. Lord knows, I can't fucking stand the majority of them. Or you can tighten up and set your family up for life. Because if you win this competition, you're not just looking at a lump sum in your bank account. Richie, you will *never* have to struggle again. What would you give to make sure Kate and your child live happily ever after? A little blood and sweat doesn't seem like too high a price, does it?"

"My life might be, though," Richie said.

"No one's supposed to die in the ring. Brutal as it might seem, there are rules that govern this game. Now, are you going to stand in the elevator for the rest of the night, or are you going to follow me?"

Richie sighed, then stepped out timidly.

Aiden nodded and walked down the corridor, prompting Richie to follow. "I know what you're thinking. We're all savages." Aiden stopped in front of a green door that looked no different than the others. He turned to Richie. "One thing you need to understand is that within the confines of these walls, within these gates, the rules of the world you've come to know have packed their bags and pissed off. I want to show you something."

He opened the door, and the room revealed on the other side appeared more like a display exhibition from a museum.

Richie followed Aiden inside, floating past stone cubic blocks propping up glass casings with books and artifacts inside—frayed, browning pages, daggers, shields, and axes with dull edges.

Aiden kept his head forward, making his way to the end of the room. "As you can see, Mr. Branadier is quite the collector."

"Yeah ... I can see that." Richie stopped at a podium with a cracked and dented scroll made of copper, perhaps. Whispers touched the rim of Richie's ear, too faint to understand. A series of breaths and hisses—

"You'll want to steer clear of that one," Aiden snapped. "You hear the whispers?"

Richie looked away. The whispers stopped. "What the fuck—"

"That scroll is rumored to steal your soul just by staring at it. It's trapped many, many souls within it for over two hundred years. Allegedly."

Richie's first instinct was to proclaim *bullshit*, but, faint as they were, he'd heard the whispers as clearly as he'd heard Aiden's voice.

"Come." Aiden waved him over to a long display at the end of the room, roughly eight feet wide with a glass top to fit its length.

Inside the glass were six empty metal stands, and next to each were discolored papers with symbols on them in ink, almost like hiero-glyphics.

"What are these? Runes?" Richie asked.

"Sure," Aiden said. "Your guess is as good as anyone else's. Bre-nadeir says they can't even be carbon dated. No one knows their origin. Some say they were here in the early days of man. Some say they were here long, long before."

"Looks like they're not here at all, though."

"Oh, the artifacts are in this building, just not here currently. You don't seem like a superstitious guy, but surely you can understand the sensitivity of such items."

Richie didn't answer. His intuition told him to leave that room. Leave that house. His raised skin told him that he was in the pres-ence of something evil. Not just the blood-hungry elites. Something otherworldly and indescribable. He followed the line of papers all the way to the right end, where three ripped papers lay in glass casings, each with graphite sketches of bulky, dark figures that might've been mistaken for apes if not for the wide white eyes and fangs. Next to the three glass casings was a podium with a closed leatherbound book. The pages jutting out from the bookends appeared to be centuries-old. Crude lines of stitching swirled around the tops and bottoms of the book, holding together the dried fragments that conjured in Richie's mind old sleepover tales of the skin-suit-wearing serial killer Ed Gein. Was it human skin holding that book together?

"The Red Demons," Aiden said. "That's the layman's term for an ancient society used for the things you see in those drawings. And the Red Demons were ruled by creatures so corrupted by pain that they removed their own skin to experience eternal sensation. Can you imagine? All of your flesh exposed all at once, that oxygen just licking at your muscle tissue. Then, to actually enjoy it? Seems barbaric, doesn't it?"

Confused, Richie didn't respond. He wasn't sure why Aiden was telling him this or why he seemed so transfixed on the display.

"According to legend, they're capable of infinite knowledge. They see beyond dimensions, unobstructed by our linear time perception. Now, I ask again: Can you imagine?" After a slight pause he said, "That book you see on the podium, that was created by the same ancient tribe who discovered them, and who, it was rumored, through trials and tribulations, was able to bring them into our world through means which we may call magic. And through that same magic, they created the Great Redeemer. The passages in that book were a contingency."

"What do you mean?" Richie asked.

"A way of destroying the Skinless Ones in case they ever decided to destroy them," Aiden said. "That's control. Human beings are flawed creatures. It's our consciousness, that very evolutionary advancement, that holds us back. We only experience time in a specific, if predictable, way. Brenadeir and men like him have the means to push the human race forward. The items in this room get us closer to understanding the realms and dimensions that we cannot access. Call it magic. Call it supernatural. I call it knowledge. But, of course, knowledge comes with consequences. Strings. When you become as powerful as William Brenadeir, the need for contingencies becomes necessary. If you open the floodgates to knowledge, you damn sure better have a back stop."

Richie watched the man speak with reverence, his eyes widening in wonder. Aiden turned those crazed eyes on Richie.

"Do you know what knowledge ultimately leads to?" Aiden asked.

Richie shook his head, knowing it was rhetorical. "Prosperity," Aiden answered. "You play the Night Games, you tap dance for all those assholes out there and put on a good show, and that's what you get. To hell with the fancy clothes and the booze and pleasantries. I hand picked you because you needed this and because I knew you could do it."

"You think you know me that well, huh?"

Aiden raised his right hand, holding his pinky finger in front of Richie's eyes. A ring of pale, rough skin ran around the bottom of it near the knuckle. "I was like you once."

Richie stared at the finger, assuming it had been cut and then sewed back on. "What am I looking at?"

"I lost a finger playing this game. Was able to get it sewn back up. Can't feel a damn thing with it, but imagine what I've gotten in return."

A horn sounded from below, reverberating from the foundation of the mansion and through the walls.

"It's time," Aiden said.

Knowledge is prosperity, Richie thought as they left the glass casings behind. After years of scraping the gutters of life, prosperity was what he yearned for—for his Kate, for his child. So he marched onward, ready for the next match, ignoring the feeling in his gut that something was very, very wrong.

Aiden had played the game and won.

How bad could it be?

11

M r. Brenadeir grabbed everyone's attention. "Now, before you four victors learn of your advantage, you will choose your opponents for head-to-head combat. Mr. Oliver Redding, you spent the longest amount of time standing on your pillar. You've earned the right to be the first to select your opponent. Will it be Mr. Wade Murrow, Mr. Vince Hines, Mr. Mason Jones, or Ms. Helena Vanderloo?"

Oliver's eyes darted to the people on the sand with him.

"I'm not gonna hurt Helena," Oliver said loud enough for the group to hear but quiet enough to hide from the crowd.

"Leave Mason for me," Shelly demanded with angry eyes.

Mason shivered on one knee as he clutched his ribs.

"Oliver, you take Wade," Tyler said through a gulp. "You two are about the same size."

"What?" Oliver scoffed. "He said head-to-head combat. Why would I pick someone my size when I could pick someone smaller than me?'

"Come on, man—" Tyler's pleas were quickly cut off when Oliver shouted:

"I choose Vince!"

"Excellent!" Mr. Brenadeir exclaimed.

Oliver had six inches on Vince and looked down at him when he said. "Nothing personal. Gotta play the game."

Vince looked up at Oliver with the ferocity of a guy who doesn't take kindly to underestimation.

Mr. Brendaier called out, "Ms. Shelly Pavia, choose your opponent—"

"Mason!" Shelly didn't hesitate.

Mr. Brenadeir laughed into the microphone. "No surprise there. Mr. Richie Stull, you're up."

Tyler rushed to Richie. "Don't leave me with Wade. He'll kill me."

"Helena told me to choose her," Richie said. "I think she knows something we don't."

Richie felt a firm hand on his shoulder. It was Helena, exhausted, but fighting to stay upright.

"You have to choose me," she told Richie. "I know what to do."

"How do you know?" Richie replied.

"*They* told me."

"What are you talking about?" Tyler stepped in. "Who told you?"

Helena worked up the strength to lift her head. "They can see us but we can't see them."

Richie was puzzled by that explanation, but Mr. Brenadeir wouldn't allow Richie too much time to think.

"Mr. Richie Stull, choose your opponent."

"Richie, if I have to fight Wade, I'll lose. I have to take care of my mom. I don't wanna die."

"You're not gonna die, okay? You're not gonna die. You have an advantage. Just make it to the next round."

Tyler nodded and flared his nostrils as he breathed deep, readying breaths. "Okay ... Okay."

Richie raised his eyes up to Mr. Brenadeir. "Helena!"

"Oh," Mr. Brenadier said. "A very intriguing choice. That leaves Mr. Tyler Grant to face Mr. Wade Murrow. The matchups are set. Now, let's present the advantage to the last round's winners. If Mr. Wade Murrow, Mr. Mason Jones, Mr. Vince Hines, and Ms. Helena Vanderloo would please make their way to the contestants' quarters."

Helena leaned in to Richie. "I'll tell you what to do."

Helena stumbled away from Richie before Vince rushed to her and helped guide her to the locker room, along with Mason. Wade took his time, waving and smiling to the cheering crowd. As the locker room doors closed on the disadvantaged contestants, the steel doors in the center of the arena began to open.

The platform methodically rose from the ground.

"Round two ... One-on-one Capture the Flag. The opponent in possession of the flag after one minute will win ten thousand dollars."

Richie's ears perked up.

"That's right," Mr Brenadeir said. "Ten thousand dollars will be deposited directly into the winner's bank accounts."

The platform halted between the contestants circling it. They looked down and saw the advantage. Hunting knives with six-inch blades were evenly placed in each direction on the table.

Mr. Brenadeir giggled through the speaker. "Our version of Capture the Flag is a twist on the classic game. See, there are multiple flags you may capture, greatly raising each competitor's chances. Each competitor will enter the arena with ten total fingers. Each of these fingers are considered flags."

"Wait, What?!" Richie shouted.

"Capture a flag within one minute, win the match. If both opponents capture the same amount of flags, this will result in a tie, and an elimination for both parties. If each competitor fails to capture at least one flag, both lose and will be eliminated."

"Woah, woah, woah!" Tyler shrieked.

The world began to spin around Richie under bloodthirsty cheers.

Mr. Brenadeir added, "Your opponents have been given the same opportunity. Now, while you four will begin with the advantage you see before you, your opponents are free to steal and overturn the advantage. Contestants, wield your weapons."

"Oh my god," Tyler shivered under the roar of the crowd. "He's gonna kill me."

"Shit," Richie mumbled to himself.

Richie ran to the wall under Mr. Brenadeir and shouted up at him, "I'll take Wade! I wanna switch! I'll take Wade!"

"The matchups are set," Mr. Brenadeir muttered with a smirk.

Tyler swiped the knife, but fumbled it, and watched it fall to the ground.

"Get a grip!" Shelly barked at Tyler as she picked up her knife. "He's all ego! You can beat him!"

Richie looked over at Oliver and saw his face go blank as he reached for the knife and clutched it. Oliver slowly brought the knife up to his eyes and turned it to watch it glimmer in the light. It was as if Oliver had shut out the chaos around him, and he and the knife were the only two things in the world. *Troubling.*

Richie trudged back to the platform and swiped his knife. The platform retracted back into the floor as the locker room doors opened.

"The first matchup is Mr. Tyler Grant versus Mr. Wade Murrow," the voice said.

"No, no, no." Tyler shrank into himself.

12

R ichie ran over to Tyler and tapped his face to force focus. "Listen to me. Hold this knife tight. Don't be loose with it. This knife is yours. Don't let him take it."

"All other contestants must leave the playing field," Mr. Brenadeir said.

"Buddy," Richie said, "you can do this, okay? You're stronger than you know. You're a survivor. You can do this."

Tyler couldn't say anything back, as no words could form amidst his fear. He nodded at Richie in diagonal motions, beads of sweat leaping off his chin.

"I'll make it easy on you!" Wade had entered the sand with his arms raised high. "Which finger do you want me to take?! Hell, I'll let you do it yourself!"

Tyler grabbed hold of Richie's shirt. "Don't leave me."

"All noncompeting contestants must leave the playing field. Any interference will result in immediate elimination."

"You can do this, okay? Be strong," Richie said before lowering his head and plodding away.

Richie joined Shelly and Oliver at the wall under Mr. Brenadeir.

Tyler's trembling hand brought the knife up to his chest as Wade inched closer to him with a sly smirk.

"People of the Red Night, are you ready?!" Mr. Brenadeir's voice blared through the speakers, eliciting a wild roar.

Wade stepped just inches from Tyler and glared down at him.

"Round two. Capture the Flag. Potential earnings: Ten thousand dollars. First matchup: Mr. Tyler Grant versus Mr. Wade Murrow."

Richie gritted his teeth and whispered to himself. "Come on, Tyler. Come on."

"One minute begins ... now.

BEEP.

Wade cocked his fist back, but Tyler was quick to make the first move. Tyler swung the knife high, missing the neck and plunging the blade into Wade's cheek. Wade stumbled backward in shock, the knife still lodged between his jaws. Wade crashed to the ground, oozing blood onto the sand. Tyler, stunned, looked over at Richie, who was just as shocked as Tyler.

A slurred masculine voice shouted from the crowd, "Get a finger! Come on!"

Tyler nodded his head and shuffled over to Wade, who was on all fours spewing blood from his mouth. Tyler reached down for the knife embedded in Wade's face. Wade launched his elbow back and blasted Tyler square in the nose. Tyler's feet kicked out from under him, and he crashed to the sand. Tyler scurried to his feet just as Wade managed to stand and face him, the knife handle protruding from one cheek and the tip of the blade protruding from the other. Wade raised an unsteady hand and grasped the handle, groaning as he pried every inch of the sharp steel from his face. Blood gushed from Wade's mouth and cheeks like a three-stream fountain.

"Thirty seconds remaining."

Wade gripped the knife tight and glared at Tyler.

"Oh, shit," Tyler uttered.

Wade dashed toward Tyler, and Tyler turned to run, but Wade lunged out and swiped the knife across Tyler's calf. Tyler shrieked with pain and crashed face first into the sand. Wade crawled over to Tyler and plunged the knife into his hamstring, sending Tyler into a screeching fit.

Richie took a step towards the playing field, but Shelly yanked him back.

"You can't," she said.

All Richie could do was watch.

"Twenty seconds."

Wade removed the knife, crawled atop Tyler's back, and stabbed the first hand he saw. He held the hand down with the knife, grabbed the pointer finger, and yanked it sideways, disconnecting it from the knuckle.

Tyler let out a tormented screech from his gut through the mixture of snot, tears, and sand caked on his mouth.

"Richie!" Tyler yelled out through tears.

Wade yanked the knife out of the hand, set the blade at the base of the limp finger, and pulled backward until the ligaments and skin ripped from the pressure of the knife.

Tyler's wide-eyed face dropped into the sand as his whole body went numb with shock.

The crowd boomed when Wade raised the mangled finger to the light.

"Ten seconds."

Wade looked down at Tyler pinned beneath him.

"Please." Tyler's sobbing voice was muffled by the red sand.

BEEP.

Wade tossed the knife and finger into the sand.

"The winner of the matchup and ten thousand dollars ... Mr. Wade Murrow!" Mr. Brenadeir declared.

The crowd became a wild volcano of deafening applause and slurs.

"A valiant effort by Mr. Tyler Grant. Unfortunately, he has been eliminated from the competition and thus will no longer be offered this opportunity. Let's have a hand for Mr. Tyler Grant!"

The crowd clapped and whistled for Tyler as he laid on the sand with a bloody hand and open wounds on his legs.

"Mr. Wade Murrow, ten thousand dollars has been transferred. Please rest on the winner's bench as we clear the playing field," Mr. Brenadeir said.

A steel bench arose from the sand by the wall across the field from Richie and the other contestants. The platform rose from the ground with three men in black suits and red, featureless masks. The platform stopped at ground level, and Wade watched as two of the men walked past him to Tyler. The other masked man grabbed the bloody knife and finger off the sand in front of Wade and retreated to the platform. Tyler squealed in pain as he was forced to his feet, the men situating themselves under his armpits. The crowd cheered once more as Tyler's limp body was carried off the field.

Tyler lifted his head to look at Richie, smiling weakly as he yelled out, "I got him, man! I got him good!"

Richie could barely hear the words, but heard them just enough. Richie nodded as Tyler was forced to the platform. Tyler and the masked men descended into the ground.

Wade, still bleeding profusely, lifted his black sweater off his bloodied, muscular torso and pressed it around his mouth from cheek to cheek. Wade took his time as he made his way to the bench. He slowly took a seat, keeping the fabric against his skin to stop the bleeding.

"Next matchup: Mr. Richie Stull versus Ms. Helena Vanderloo."

13

Richie sighed as he looked down at his knife. He trudged away from the wall and towards the middle of the floor. The locker room doors opened, and Helena walked through them upright with her head held high. She had a focus in her eyes like she was operating with full conviction, an odd switch, Richie thought, since she'd been vomiting and in and out of consciousness just moments before. Helena walked up to Richie, keeping a yard between them, and nodded to him.

"People of the Red Night, are you ready for more?!" Mr. Brenadeir shouted.

A wave of roars blasted over Richie and Helena.

"You're not gonna like what I say next," Helena said.

"What is it?" Richie asked.

"You need to kill me."

"... What?"

"I can take down the game from the other side."

Richie shook his head. "The other side?"

"One minute begins ... now."

BEEP.

The applause amplified as Helena spoke fast. "People who have died in this game are trapped in another dimension, but they told me about an in-between you pass through before you get there. I can help you from there, and we can end this together. But you have to kill me."

"What? I don't—"

"I know my stepmom killed my father. I know she invited me here to die so I would stop digging into it. I'm not making it out alive. Kill me."

"I ... I ..." Richie stuttered.

"Running out of time."

Helena grabbed Richie's knife-wielding hand and, with no hesitation, plunged the knife into her heart, Richie's hand still on the handle.

"Woah, woah!" Richie shouted in bewilderment, too startled to resist.

Helena kept her firm hold on Richie's lame hand as she retracted the knife from her chest and plunged it in again, taking advantage of Richie's shock.

"Thirty seconds remaining."

Richie yanked his hand free of her grasp and fell backwards onto the sand.

Helena twisted the knife in her heart and fell to her knees. She tried to pull the knife out with one hand, but it was trapped between bones. Blood poured from her mouth as she brought both hands to the knife and wrestled it out of her. Blood was gathering beneath rapidly.

She choked as she waved Richie over. "Come ... here."

Richie sprang to his feet and bolted over to Helena.

Helena wheezed as she rested her quivering forehead onto his. Then ...

Total darkness. Richie's world went pitch black.

Richie slowly rose and saw that he was standing on a black floor surrounded by dark, endless nothingness. He twisted his head around wildly, searching for anything around him, until he saw a faint glow in the distance. With trepidation, he inched towards the pebble of light. As he came closer, an image began to form. He stopped before a shimmering barrier between the dark space and an image of him on one knee, looking down at a lifeless, bloody Helena on the sand of the coliseum.

A distant roar sounded behind Richie. He turned and saw nothing in the darkness. Roars grew louder, noises he had never heard an animal make. Chains rattled. Large feet stomped. Whimpering, screeching voices cried out for help.

Helena suddenly appeared directly in front of him. "It worked."

He leapt backward, startled.

Richie found himself gazing up at a bright light, a high-pitched buzz ringing in his ears. He wiggled his fingers to feel sand. His stomach plummeted with the realization that he was back on the playing field. His other hand was open with a lightweight object in the palm. He sat up and brought the object to his face ... a severed pale finger with black nail polish. Helena was lying dead beside him. The buzzing in his ears began to fade, slowly allowing the roars of the blood-thirsty crowd to blanket him.

"The winner of the matchup is Mr. Richie Stull!" Mr. Brenadeir declared. "And while Ms. Helena Vanderloo did the heavy lifting in her death, rules are rules. Mr. Richie Stull has earned ten thousand dollars!"

Applause all around for Richie, who was seemingly unfazed by the sound of the money he had won. He looked down at Helena's blood-soaked corpse, devastated by her death, dazed by his trip to the dark place.

The platform rose, and the masked men did their duties, retrieving the knife, the finger, and Helena's body before disappearing back into the ground.

Richie stood up and slowly looked around.

"Helena?" Richie murmured. "Can you hear me?"

He received nothing in return.

"Mr. Richie Stull," Mr. Brenadeir said. "A total of ten thousand dollars has been transferred. Congratulations. Please, rest at the winner's bench."

Richie trudged to the bench where Wade was sitting on one end, still applying pressure to his gashed cheeks. Richie went to the other end and took a seat. Wade turned his head to Richie.

"You didn't do anything to earn that." Wade's voice was muffled through the shirt over his mouth.

Richie had nothing to respond with. His hands were bloody, his mouth was agape, and his head was spinning.

"Next matchup: Ms. Shelly Pavia versus Mr. Mason Jones."

14

S helly made her way to the middle of the sand, gripping her knife with a no-bullshit stare. The locker room doors opened, and Mason sheepishly waddled towards her. He had left his tie and suit jacket behind, donning a shirt with sweat stains so large they had fused into one large upper body stain. He walked a few feet onto the sand and stopped, leaving a large gap between them.

"Listen to me!" Mason shouted. "If you let me win, I'll give you half. And half of the rest of my earnings from the rest of the game! We could both get out of here with a shitload of money!"

Shelly scoffed and moved closer to Mason. "Did you come up with that deal when you were beating me over the back with a stick? You're a snake. I don't like snakes."

"People of the Red Night," Mr. Brenadeir belted out. "Are you ready for your next matchup?!"

"*One minute begins ... now.*"

BEEP.

Mason held his fists up to his chin, and Shelly moved within feet of him.

"I'm just gonna take a finger," she said. "Don't make me have to do more than that."

Mason suddenly dropped to his knees.

"Oh, please!" Mason sobbed. "Please don't hurt me! Oh, please!"

Shelly loosened up slightly. Then, Mason lunged at Shelly, wrapping himself around her, pinning her arms to her sides, and drove her into the ground. He mounted her stomach and pressed his knee to the wrist of her knife hand, dropping all his weight into it, until her hand released the knife. He grabbed the knife and slammed it down toward Shelly, but she freed her other hand, held it in front of her chest, and the blade shot through the palm. Shelly's hand kept the knife's point hovering just over her chest. Mason shifted his weight, and he tried to shove the blade down, allowing Shelly to free her other hand and send a fist crashing across Mason's jaw. Mason rolled off of Shelly in a daze, leaving the knife lodged in Shelly's hand. Shelly yanked the knife out, crawled to Mason, who was fully exposed on his back, and slammed her good hand into his mouth with a crunch. She jolted her fist into his nose, pulverizing it. Mason was out cold.

"Thirty seconds remaining."

Shelly took the knife, pressed the blade to Mason's pinky, and carved until the finger was severed. She held the finger up, causing a riotous wave of cheers.

Exhausted, Shelly held onto the finger, dropped the knife, and staggered away from Mason, towards the winner's bench.

"Fifteen seconds remaining."

Richie locked eyes with Shelly as she made her way through the sand. Then he saw movement behind her. Mason had come to. Richie quickly stood up. Shelly turned around and saw Mason charging her with the knife. She raised her forearm to shield her face, and he slashed across it. Shelly backpedaled as blood dripped from her arm.

"Ten seconds remaining."

"I'll kill you!" Mason garbled through shattered teeth.

Blinded by his own blood, Mason swiped at her again, but stumbled and fell to the ground, dropping the knife.

Shelly placed a knee on the back of Mason's head, forcing his face into the sand.

"Five seconds remaining."

Mason squirmed as he fought for air. His hand searched for the knife in the sand, but Shelly grabbed it and tossed it away.

BEEP.

Shelly let off of Mason, allowing him to roll over and gasp for air.

"And the winner is Ms. Shelly Pavia!" Mr. Brenadeir shouted as the crowd quaked. "A formidable contestant indeed. Ten thousand dollars has been transferred. Congratulations. Please, rest on the winner's bench."

Shelly dropped the finger and walked away from Mason, grasping her bloody hand. Richie took off his tie and offered it to her.

"Thanks." She took a seat and wrapped the tie around her wounded hand. "Why did she do it?"

"Helena?" Richie sat beside her.

"She told you something before she did it. What did she say?"

"… I'm still trying to make sense of it."

"Listen to me," Shelly said. "I got a kid. She's the only good thing I've ever done. She needs a mother that doesn't put her through the hell I went through with my parents. She has no one besides me. If I don't come home, she goes into the foster system. I gotta get back to her. You have a kid on the way, yeah?"

Richie nodded his head.

"You help me get through this, then I'll help *you* get through this," Shelly said. "Deal?"

"Yeah … Deal."

"Final matchup: Mr. Oliver Redding versus Mr. Vince Hines."

15

Vince stepped onto the sand with every muscle in his body tense, ready to brawl. He was outsized, but that didn't seem to bother him. He had the look of a fighter. The man staring back at him gripping a knife was a different Oliver—shoulders caved in, blank eyes, lost in a flurry of thoughts. Vince rolled up his sleeves as he came closer to the middle of the field.

"Nothing personal here," Vince said with sorrow. "My family needs the money."

"I've seen death," Oliver mumbled.

"What?" Vince didn't know if he'd heard that right.

"They told me what would happen if I left," Oliver spoke with his face to the ground, as if Vince wasn't there. "This is my punishment. And now ... I have to do their will."

Vince cocked his head, perplexed. Fear suddenly started to show as he stood in front of Oliver. He slowly raised his fists.

"One minute begins ... now."

"Forgive me," Oliver said.

"Just fight." Vince stood firm in a fighter's stance, ready for action.

Vince saw that Oliver wasn't budging from his cold, odd posture. Vince bounced on his feet, readying himself to throw a blow at Oliver's unguarded face. Vince jabbed into Oliver's nose, and Oliver's head recoiled from the blow. Vince jabbed him again to the same effect, forcing Oliver to take a step back. Still, Oliver was unflinching. Vince looked down at the knife held at Oliver's side. If Oliver was giving him the game, he was taking it. Vince lunged for the knife in Oliver's hand—

SLICE.

Oliver slashed the knife across Vince's throat.

Vince turned to stone, stunned, blood beginning to slide out of the gash in his neck. He wheezed for air as he backed away. The trickling blood began to pour. He brought his hands to his neck to stop the blood, but the opening was too large, and blood spewed over his hands and through his fingers. Vince crashed to his knees, all color fleeing his face.

"Thirty seconds remaining."

Oliver's heavy steps pounded the sand as he stood over Vince. Vince held a desperate hand up to Oliver. Oliver wrapped his hand around Vince's palm and squeezed it tight. He reeled the knife above his head and slammed the blade down into Vince's wrist. The blow wasn't enough to sever the hand, so Oliver drove the blade into his wrist again and again and again until the wrist was limp enough to pry the broken bones away from the arm.

Vince fell to the ground, life leaving his body rapidly.

"Ten seconds remaining."

Vince coughed up his last bloody breath as Oliver stared at the sand at his feet, nothing behind his eyes.

BEEP.

The crowd exploded with delight at what Oliver had done. Oliver's vicious actions were undoubtedly the highlight of the night.

"What a show, Mr. Oliver Redding!" Mr. Brenadeir declared amidst the uproarious crowd. "The matchup's champion and winner of ... Well, he took the whole hand, didn't he? Let's say ten for each finger, bringing him to a grand total of fifty thousand dollars!"

Richie viewed the scene in horror as Oliver dropped the hand, then the knife. Oliver stood still in the sand, showing no emotion, even as the masked men surfaced, retrieved the knife and hand, and dragged Vince's body away.

"Congratulations, winning contestants!" Mr. Brenadeir's voice rang out. "You have earned the opportunity to move forward. Please come to the center of the playing field."

Richie sat on the steel bench with his head hung low. He looked over at Wade, who was staring boldly back at him. Wade removed his shirt from his face and threw it on the sand, displaying slices with dried blood on either side of his red mouth. Wade got to his feet, stretched his bare chest out wide, and roamed away from the bench.

Shelly patted Richie on the back. "Let's go."

Shelly walked away as Richie rose.

"Can you hear me?' Helena's voice crackled in his ears like a static hiss, startling Richie, dropping him back to the bench.

"Helena?" He looked all around, disoriented.

"I connected to you," Helena's disembodied voice said. "You're a receiver for as long as I'm able to stay in the in-between. You can hear but can't talk back. Nod if you can hear me."

Richie nodded, still looking every which way.

"Okay," Helena said. "Let's destroy these assholes."

PART

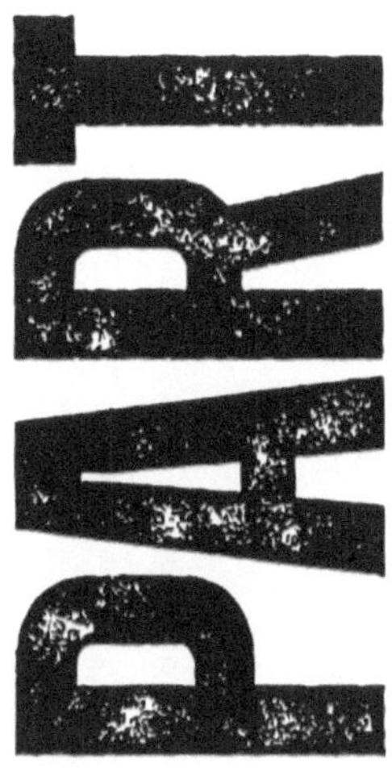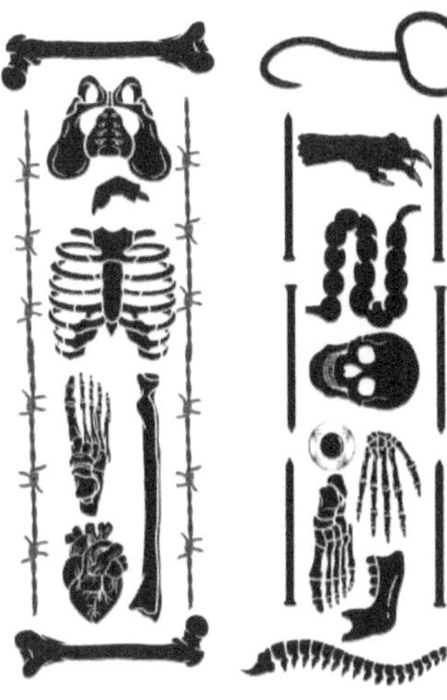

GO TO HELL

WRITTEN BY

JOEY POWELL

16

It was only once he'd crossed the threshold from the arena to the waiting room, once the excited shrieks of a carnage-seeking crowd of wealthy elites faded out of his orbit and his feet pressed against the cold assortment of stone, that Richie's hands felt heavy from the blood on them. It was thick and resilient like honey, and no matter how hard he attempted to rub the red off on his thrift-store dress pants, the remnants of Helena remained on his trembling fingers.

Helena was dead. She was dead because she'd chosen to be. She'd plunged the knife into her skin with the ease with which she might've sliced through a piece of fruit. He could still hear her voice in his head like a ringing of tinnitus. So clear for a few short seconds after she'd passed, and then gone.

She'd claimed she could communicate with the dead.

And that was goddamn impossible. Richie may have just facilitated the death of someone delusional and in need of serious help.

Shelly nudged him on her way in. "Toughen up, yeah?"

At the center of the crest, a woman in an old-timey nurse's outfit complete with a silly hat gave Richie and the contestants filing in behind him a wave. She had to have been around the same age as Richie, but had that sagging-skin look that Richie knew well in his short lifetime of hopping around between odd jobs. Rapid aging caused by drugs, alcohol, or maybe some combination. The sight of her in the outfit was surreal, as if he'd fallen out of a Roman colosseum and into a

1950s black and white flick. Next to her was a rolling cart with medical supplies—bandages, needles, scissors, and the like.

The young woman smiled. "My name is Raven. I'm here to address any injuries you all may have." She snuck a sly look at Wade and said, "I see you're in need of some medical attention, dear."

"No shit," Wade said. "I had a knife go through one end of my face and out the other."

"Oh, you poor thing." Raven approached Wade and put her smooth hands under his chin, making a spectacle of her inspection. "Clean in and out. You were lucky it didn't hit bone."

"Yeah, real lucky, babe."

"Why don't you all have a seat?" Raven said. "I'll tend to each of you after I clean these wounds."

Richie gladly followed her suggestion. Though he'd made out better than most in the room, save for the stinger on his shoulder, he felt exhausted. Must've been the adrenaline purge, that come down from the fight or flight response, his mind signaling to his body that he was okay now. He knew that wouldn't last for long, though.

The double doors converged, closing them in and swallowing Richie's view of the sand pit arena. He knew it wouldn't be long until he was out there again, and his mind raced wondering what the next "competition" would be. What would he have to do to secure his family's future? Even if he wanted to quit now, how long would ten thousand dollars last him? Forget the rent payments, how expensive would giving birth be if he didn't have insurance when the baby came?

He'd witnessed death. He'd been inches away from it, close enough for his breath to touch Helena's cheek before she bled out. What if he didn't survive the game? What if Kate was left to raise a child on her own? Richie might've been an actual fuck up or just a victim of circumstance but knew in his heart that the child wouldn't be better off without him, even if Richie had left him a large sum of money in his wake. Regardless of what he did tonight, Richie had an opportunity to leave his old ways—his old life—behind. To be better.

The risk-reward ratio was clear. He had no choice but to keep going.

"The others that came in before us," Richie called out to Raven. "Where are they?"

"I'm not sure who you're referring to, dear," Raven answered as she pressed rags to either side of Wade's face. "I've only been here for a few minutes. I wouldn't have seen anyone else."

"Worried about your boyfriend?" Wade winced as his cheeks rubbed against the rags.

"Keep still," Raven said. "I have to clean you up before I sew the wounds."

"With those hands? You're shaking worse than my grandma," Wade said. "What the hell is that, cataracts?"

"She's helping you, Wade," Shelly said from her bench. "I'd be grateful. Way your cheeks look now, someone could reach in and rip a handful of tongue out."

"Is that someone going to be you?" Wade shot back.

"Do you ever shut up?" Oliver's voice carried a heft to it, a dominance that silenced everyone. Even Wade.

Two people thus far had died in the ring, but out of all the victors sitting there in the circle, only Oliver had intentionally, callously, ended someone's life.

"I apologize, dear." Raven fumbled the blood-soaked rags and placed them in the lower tier of the rolling cart. "The shaking should not be happening. I'll get that fixed." She walked over to the elevator and pressed the up button, then turned and gave the group a close-lipped smile as she waited.

When the elevator doors opened, a woman with piercing green eyes and ivory skin stood on the other side, hair straightened and bobbing overtop the shoulders of an emerald suit jacket.

Raven said, "Oh, hello, Miss—"

"Out of my fucking way." The woman shoved Raven effortlessly, her broad shoulders and tall stature dominant.

Her eyes found Richie, and as soon as they did, her index finger straightened out toward him like the barrel of a gun. "You!" She marched forward. "You fucking degenerate."

Richie stood, readying himself for an impending attack, his cortisol kicking in once again.

"Stop right there, Darlene!" It was Aiden's voice, coming from the double doors Richie and his peers had just walked through. He twisted his body to the side, squeezing through the double door so quickly, the button securing his jacket popped off.

But the woman didn't stop.

Darlene Vanderloo? Richie thought.

Wade laughed, coming to the same conclusion. "Oh shit."

In his confused state, Richie failed to swat away the hands of Helena's mother, and so they came toward him unimpeded, wrapping around Richie's throat faster than he could react. The grip was tighter than he'd expected. The woman was taller than him by about two inches and outweighed him by about forty pounds.

He kept his feet planted, refusing to go to the ground like she so obviously wanted.

"Get the hell off of him!" Aiden sprang into action, grappling with Darlene's hands and pulling them away.

Richie gasped. "I didn't kill your daughter."

"To hell with your words, you filth!" Darline shouted as Aiden held her back like a kid in a schoolyard fight.

"She held my hands and stabbed herself!" Richie screamed.

"You saw what happened, Darlene," Aiden said. "Everyone in that crowd did." He pushed her away. "You just have to come to terms with the fact that you drove your daughter to suicide."

Darlene aimed that damning index finger at Aiden. "Oh, you son of a bitch. You recruited this fucking animal and you're going to blame *my daughter* for what happens now? The next one to die is going to be him!"

"Miss Vanderloo." Brenadeir's voice sounded from above, echoing through the room and causing everyone inside of it to look up.

Richie hadn't noticed it before—the black half-globe on the ceiling in the corner of the room. A security camera.

"You've clearly forgotten the rules, so I'll remind you," Brenadeir's disembodied voice continued. "Should you endanger any one of our guests outside of the competition, you will forfeit your chance at winning."

"Go to hell, William!" Darline shrieked at the camera. "If you think I'm participating in this rat race, you can kiss my ass!"

"Have you made the decision to forfeit?"

Silence.

"Then I suggest you sit down with your fellow … *contestants.*"

With one last cold look at Richie, Darline did as instructed. She found a vacant stone bench and perched down on it, removing her suit jacket, then her heels. As she rolled up the sleeves of her satin blouse, she said, "Could I at least get some tennis shoes delivered?"

"Certainly, Miss Vanderloo," Brenadeir replied through the camera speaker.

The group shared confused looks as Darlene finished rolling the second sleeve to her elbow. Aiden remained standing in the center of the room, hands on his hips.

"What's going on?" Richie asked.

Aiden sighed. "I told you, Richie ... No one is supposed to die in the games. The rules we agree to when we sponsor a contestant ..." He glanced at Darlene. "... is that we as sponsors take the place of our champions should they die. So now Darlene Vanderloo is forced to take the place of Helena." He then looked at Oliver. "I suspect someone's going to be very upset with you as well. If I had to guess, Vince's sponsor is trying to weasel his way out of the game as we speak."

Wade gave another bloody laugh.

"You think this is funny?" Darlene snapped at Wade.

"That you would make your own daughter play this game? Yeah, a little bit. That she'd kill herself just to put *you* in the game. I mean, come on ... that's just bittersweet irony, isn't it?"

Darlene shot up.

"Careful," Shelly said. "Not sure what happens when you forfeit, but the way you rolled over like a dog when Brenadeir threatened forfeiture, I can only assume it isn't good. Welcome to the games, bitch. You're one of us now."

"One of *you*?" Darlene spat. "Do you have any idea how hard I've worked to be *nothing* like you?"

Oliver spoke. "Twenty-five years ago you fucked a CEO." All heads turned to the quiet killer. "Then you had him killed so you could take over his company. Allegedly."

"You don't know what you're talking about. I loved my husband, you gutter trash. I helped him build his company while you were swimming around in dumpsters looking for trailer furniture."

"Darlene! Enough!" Aiden yelled, silencing the group. He paced, rubbing his fingers against his skull in audible feverish scratches. "Richie ... let's go chat."

17

The elevator ride up was familiar and silent. Familiar as it was, though, this time the tension was heavier, threatening to crush Richie's chest, to puncture his lungs. He hated the man next to him.

"Lost a finger in the games, huh?" Richie said.

"My opponent lost two," Aiden replied. "Let's get that blood off your hands."

The two of them sat in leather chairs opposite each other next to an unlit fireplace. Books lined the walls from floor to ceiling.

Richie's hands were clean, but his clothes weren't. Every time he inhaled, that metallic smell of blood wafted deep into his nostrils, thick as cigarette smoke.

After a long moment of silence, Aiden spoke. "Nice girl, Raven. You notice anything unique about her?"

"Besides the 1950s nurse cosplay?"

Aiden chuckled. Richie had grown to hate that sound and would prefer having tacks shoved in his ears if it meant he could stop hearing it.

"Brenadeir does enjoy tradition," Aiden said. "The old ways give him comfort. He's older than he looks."

"He looks pretty fuckin' old."

"You'd be wise to not speak ill of him."

"Just an observation."

Aiden eased back in his chair. "Well, you're not wrong. However old you think he is, he's older than that. Perks of being filthy rich."

Another lengthy silence grew between them.

"Her hands were shaking," Richie said. "Raven, that is. Either it's a condition or withdrawals. Based on the skin degeneration, I'm guessing she went cold turkey on something pretty recently."

Aiden smiled. "Very astute. Raven is a nurse practitioner. Also a single mother. She was put in the unfortunate position of working overtime to make ends meet. When you work sixteen-hour days for weeks on end, eventually you need something to keep you alert. Mr. Brenadeir plucked Raven out of obscurity when she was at her lowest point. As an addict, she'd lost her house, her child, her job. Now, she lives here, her child's education is paid for, and she's doing what she's good at."

"Sewing up prize fighters is a noble profession."

"Drop the sarcasm."

"I watched two people die tonight. Sorry if I'm not feeling all that chipper."

"I'll say again: No one's expected to die in the ring. Two people dying in one round ... That's unprecedented. It's never happened before."

"Where are the ones who lost?"

Aiden grunted. "Don't bother yourself with them. They're fine. But that shaking you saw in Raven's hands? That's not withdrawal symptoms. She's undergone an experimental procedure that'll take years of red tape before it gets to public consumption, if it ever does. It helps control her levels of dopamine, melatonin, and norepinephrine. She had undiagnosed bipolar disorder that went untreated for years. Pair that with a bit of nose candy and heightened levels of cortisol and skyrocketing blood pressure ... She was an absolute mess. Turn a dial and she's happy again. Turn another dial and her anxiety is gone. It requires some serious monitoring, but I'll be damned if it doesn't work."

"Sounds dangerous."

"Anything that disrupts sounds dangerous at first. As I told you before, the rules of the world you've come to know have packed their fucking bags. You need to get used to that or you won't survive the next round."

"Worried that you might end up in the game?"

Aiden clenched his jaw. "I need you to listen very carefully. Whether you intended it or not, Darlene Vanderloo is a callous little cunt, and she *will* hold her daughter's death against you and, by extension, me. She will try to kill you in order to get my ass in the game."

"Are you saying I have to kill her before she kills me?"

"No. Under no circumstances can you do that. There *must* be six losers alive for there to be one winner."

"And if there isn't?"

"Everyone gets nothing."

The horn blared from down below, signaling the start of the next match.

18

T he exit doors to the waiting room were open when Richie returned to it, with crowd chatter seeping in. His fellow contestants were gone.

Aiden stayed put on the elevator, giving Richie a gentle nudge on his back. "Go get 'em, champ. Remember: this is for your family. For—"

"—Prosperity."

The elevator doors closed behind Richie as he walked past the empty stone benches and into the amber glow of the arena lights. Guests eagerly huddled over the railing of the rafters twenty feet in the air. A digital clock hung from the ceiling. Richie couldn't help but feel like this was some kind of star entrance at a sporting event. All that was missing were the pops of fireworks and a long tunnel.

The remaining contestants stood in the center of the arena. The looks on each of them—a mix of nerves, disgust, fear—made Richie feel an even higher degree of anxiety. Even the bravado on Wade's sewn-up face was a mask. Behind the inflamed skin surrounding the stitches, the pointed brows, the clenched jaw, Wade was wondering what he would have to do next and to whom.

Darlene Vanderloo cut Richie down with her serpentine eyes. Having replaced the heels with sneakers, she was closer to his height, but, still, he didn't want to think about those strong hands clutching at his neck again. Whatever happened next, he'd have to keep one eye on her.

Next to Darlene was a short, round man in suspenders, dress pants, and leather loafers. His hair plugs had been set too high, giving his wispy brown hair the appearance of a hay field. Vince's sponsor, no doubt. Would he seek retribution against Oliver? Doubtful. Head-to-head, the two were a complete mismatch.

Richie stepped onto the battlefield, glancing at the steel rectangular structure at the far end of it. The steel frame was lined with stones, all of which had a symbol on them. He squinted at those symbols plastered on the surfaces. They were a similar style to the symbols he'd just seen inside the glass casing in Brenadeir's museum of strange artifacts.

No ... They *were* the missing artifacts from that room Richie had so desperately wanted to leave. The stones that were meant to be placed on the vacant stands. Instead, they were there on the platform twenty-five yards away from Richie. Wires snaked around the edges of the frame, swirling into one mass that connected the frame to a metal booth outside the ring where the two men in white hazmat suits stood idly. Inside the booth was a series of glowing buttons and dials and levers. On the outside, an interconnected circle of humming generators.

Whatever happens—

"What?" Richie twisted his head. It was Helena's voice again, clear and sharp as if she were whispering straight into his ear.

—believe what you're seeing.

"Helena?" Richie whispered, rotating in a full circle before stopping. Wade, Oliver, and Shelly stared in confusion.

Believe everything, Helena said.

"The fuck?" Richie whispered.

"Is he talkin' to himself?" Wade asked.

Remember that they're weak, Helena said.

Richie straightened himself up and walked toward the center of the circle to join the others.

"Come on, Richie Rich," Wade said. "Everyone's waiting on you."

He joined the line, temporarily touching shoulders with Shelly, who said, "You okay there? Looked like you were goin' schizo on us for a second."

"Just ... thought I'd heard something," Richie said.

Richie eyed the crowd behind him, finding Aiden perched up behind the railing. They locked eyes, and Aiden raised his pinky finger. A shallow attempt at solidarity.

"Ladies and gentlemen," Brenadeir's voice stabbed through the speakers. He stood above them in his small suite like a Roman emperor sans robe, dousing the microphone in his saliva. "All of you here now have shown loyalty. You've paid handsomely ..."

Giggles sounded from the stands.

"And what you get to see here tonight is unlike anything you'll ever see. A treatise between people. Between worlds."

"What the fuck is this guy on about?" Wade whispered.

"Just listen, you twat," Darlene said.

Brenadeir continued. "We now have two new members in the ring. Miss Darlene Vanderloo and Mr. Arnold Swanson."

The man in the suspenders—Arnold—let out a nervous breath.

"Before revealing what the next round entails, let's bring out a special guest." Brenadeir turned, creating space near the middle of his stage, waving his arm to someone behind him.

Clapping. Howls. Joyful screams. The crowd knew who this guest of honor was.

Richie expected another tight-skinned man with a three-hundred-dollar haircut and studded cufflinks. But as the figure walked into the light, as the cheering grew louder, Richie knew this human being wasn't like the rest of the elites he'd met today. He may not have been an elite at all. For one, he was young—maybe Richie's age—and he didn't have that same plastic grin as the others. He was somber. No pride. All remorse.

"Please welcome Jackson Dawkins!" Brenadeir shouted into the mic.

And welcome him the crowd did.

"You'll remember Jackson as the most recent winner of the Night Games," Brenaider said. "An activist turned eco terrorist who ran into some legal trouble. Jackson would still be in prison now if we hadn't stepped in. What do you have to say for yourself, Mr. Dawkins?"

He handed the microphone to Jackson. After a few long, silent seconds, he said, "Thank you, Mr. Brendier," like a dog thankful for table scraps.

Brenadeir brought the microphone back to his lips. "Such a good kid. Now, for this next round, Mr. Dawkins will have the pleasure of sponsoring a winner. And that winner will have an advantage in the next round. Yes, that's right. We want a show."

Double doors opened ahead of Richie. Two men in suits rolled out a large steel box the size of a small camper into the center of the ring. They unlatched the sides and let the heavy side gate fall dramatically.

Weapons.

"The next game is tug-of-war ..." Brenadeir side-eyed Darlene and the short man. "... with a twist! The winning side is measured in the amount of blood."

Over the crowd noise, Arnold pleaded with the other contestants. "Protect me and I'll make sure you all leave here rich."

Darlene chuckled. "Drop the act. Not a single one of them is leaving this place."

The ground moved beneath them, rising up as the sand shuffled below their feet. Gears and hydraulics whined.

Eventually, all that was left was a floor of metal grating like that of a clanky warehouse platform. With the sand removed, the metal became clear. One half of the circle was colored black, and the other half was colored white. And still they continued to rise.

19

"What the fuck did she just say?" Wade shouted as the platform slowed to a stop.

Darlene continued to laugh. "If you knew what was waiting at the end of this, you would know that death is a better outcome."

"Can it, Darlene!" Arnold commanded.

"Not my fault you backed the wrong horse. One look at that house of cards and I would've told you he'd shit himself the minute the knives came out."

Wade stepped toward Darlene. "What do you mean none of us are leaving?"

"She's drunk as always," Arnold answered. "Don't let her belligerence get in your head. Whatever your winnings are here, I'll goddamn quadruple it."

"Silence!" Brenadeir ordered the crowd. "It appears we have some infighting among our group. You'll want to reconcile your differences now before the next game begins."

"Oh, fuck off," Darlene said under her breath.

They were now suspended ten feet in the air. Richie looked through the metal gaps in the flooring below and only saw more metal.

The weapons chamber remained in the middle of the platform. Blades and gunmetal shimmered under the overhead lights.

Another chorus of gears grinding sounded around them. Thick glass went up behind the railing of the seating area.

"Choose your weapon as I explain the rules," Brenadeir said.

Darlene was the first to rush toward the chamber. "One each!" Brenadeir added.

A few seconds later, a 9mm was nestled in her thick palm. She took a shooter's stance, straightened her arms, looked down the sights.

The rich do love their guns, Richie thought as he walked with the rest of the group over to the chamber to inspect the weapons. Arnold promptly snatched up the Uzi.

Richie took in the inventory. A machete. A scythe. A katana. A goddamn chainsaw.

One thing he didn't see was extra ammo for the two guns.

"What, are we all gonna kill each other now?" Richie asked to anyone within earshot.

Darlene released the magazine and inspected it, counting her shots. "Wait till you see our opponents."

"In the middle of the circle, you will see a dividing line," Brenadeir said. "You are designated as the black team. The white team will be here momentarily."

Shelly took a swing of the katana. She noticed Richie eyeing her. "You better arm up."

Long range, Helena whispered in his ear.

"Huh?"

"I said you better arm up," Shelly repeated.

Richie nodded.

Something to keep your distance, Helena said.

Richie spotted Wade twirling a pair of sais, living out his boyhood dream of being a Ninja Turtle, no doubt. When Richie checked the armory again, his eyes landed on a broadsword with a jewel at the bottom of the handle. Scratched and sharpened. Battle tested. Something that would look appropriate in the hands of Arnold Schwarzenegger in *Conan the Barbarian*.

"Got it," Richie said aloud.

He reached over and lifted it off the two hooks it was perched on. The weight of it took him by surprise, and he clenched his forearms in resistance.

"You sure you can handle that thing?" Wade asked with a grin, holding a sai in each hand. The logic was clear—two blades are better than one. But he didn't have a dead girl in his ear to tell him how bad of an idea that was.

"I guess we'll find out," Richie said. He held the sword upright, both hands on the grip, blade toward the ceiling in a posture that made him feel powerful.

"If everyone's settled," Brenadeir said, "step away from the dividing line and we'll await the white team's arrival."

They lined up again and waited.

"What now?" Richie whispered.

Believe everything you see, Helena said.

Brenadeir looked away from the contestants and toward the metal booth where the two men in white hazmat suits awaited his command. One man raised his hand above a dashboard of glowing buttons and dials and placed it on a metal lever.

"Jumpstart the gate, if you will," Brenadeir said.

One man pulled the lever. A series of electric squeaks fed through the generators surrounding the booth, feeding power through the entangled stream of wires all the way to the square steel frame enclosed by stones.

Richie thought it was a trick of the eye at first, that green flicker popping off a symbol on one of the stones. A reflection of the light, perhaps. But when all of the symbols faded from a natural black and specs of green began growing within them, it was undeniable.

The rocks were glowing.

20

A metal clank made Richie jump.

"What … the … fuck." Shelly's grip had gone slack, and she'd dropped her katana as a result.

It was the only reasonable response. Richie had to remind himself of what Helena had told him. He had to remember to believe his eyes, because what he was seeing now was absolutely not possible.

The edges of the steel rectangle materialized into a glowing pane of black, slowly converging at the center like a Polaroid developing.

Darlene laughed that same cynical laugh, then pulled back the slide of her 9mm to check the chamber.

The crowd chatter died down, and for a tense minute and a half, the soundtrack of the evening chaos was the hum of the generators shotgunning volt after volt of electricity into the frame, somehow powering the glowing rocks. The murky black film shimmered within the frame, wobbling like a sail in a calm breeze.

And then, something reached through it.

Fingers …

No—claws.

The hand and the arm that followed looked humanoid, but in a bright, sunburned red, with thick, yellow fingers taking the lead.

Inch by inch, some*thing* came through the portal. A ropey, sexless thing that may have once been human, with a smooth head, a smooth crotch, and skin so tight it was almost completely transparent, showing every ripple of muscle tissue underneath. The thing's eyes were wide open, dried and red along the edges, and its lips were gone. With nothing to conceal its teeth, it looked upon the crowd with a skeletal smile, stepping slowly, tiredly away from the threshold, away from whatever hellish world it had come from. It didn't react when the crowd cheered for it.

Neither did the second nor the third thing. Nor the other nine that came out of the shimmer, each tearing through the fabric of reality slowly like newborns from a womb.

All the while, the contestants remained still. All except Darlene, who snapped greedy little glances at each of them, taking in their reactions.

Shelly bent down and picked up her katana, then turned to Richie. "You're seeing this too, right?"

All Richie could respond with in return was what Helena had told him. "They're weaker than they look."

"What? You know what these things are?"

"No."

"You have three minutes," Brenadeir said into the microphone. "At the end of three minutes, we will calculate the weight of blood accumulated on each side. The side with the most blood wins."

"So we have to bring them over to our side and slice them up?" There was a breathless quality to Richie's speech, as if his words were trying to catch up with what his brain was registering.

"Doesn't seem like it matters whose blood it is," Shelly said. "So long as we have more on our side at the end of this."

Richie tightened his grip, digging the handle of the sword into his palm. He looked over at Wade, who looked his way as well, regarding the longsword in comparison to his tiny little ninja knives. Wade mouthed, *Fuck*.

Past Wade, Oliver held a double-bitted battle axe over his shoulder with Nordic inscriptions on it. Richie tried to discern the look on his face—concern, confusion. One thing it wasn't was fear. It was as if he'd come here planning to die. And that meant he was a good player to keep close.

The reddish things sniffed ... sniffed ... sniffed ...

As their faded eyes wandered, it became clear they couldn't see. With their nostrils pointed upward, their toes slowly crept toward Richie and his now-teammates.

"What the fuck are these things?" Wade asked.

Arnold raised his Uzi, tucking the backside in the meat of his shoulder. "Meet the Red Demons."

"Get ready ..." Brenadeir announced.

The LED screen above them lit up with "3:00."

The Red Demons walked faster, their blurred eyes aimed at their opponents. At Richie.

One of them shrieked through rotted teeth.

For the first time, Richie considered that he might not be making it home. That he might not live to see his child. That he'd be killed at the hands of these beasts, and he would vanish. Tomorrow morning, Kate would wake up without him beside her. After a flood of missed calls and unanswered texts, she'd call the police. She'd tell them about Aiden Prince. Aiden would deny seeing Richie. Richie would never be found, buried in the rubble of this twisted sport.

Out of his periphery, Richie felt Darlene Vanderloo's eyes on him and considered that she was rationing a bullet for his skull. Maybe she would make things easy on him and delay the inevitable.

No, he thought. This wasn't the time to get sad. It wasn't the time to plan out his eulogy. He'd been duped. Scammed. Manipulated by the people who manipulate for pleasure and out of boredom. He wasn't afraid for the life he might lose; Richie was pissed at the life *they* wanted to take from him. *They*. The Darlene Vanderloos and Aiden Princes and William Brenadeirs of the world.

As long as he had fight left in him, he'd stay alive just to spite them. And he had a fucking Conan sword to pair with his rage.

With Shelly between him and Darlene, Richie whispered, "You're gonna wanna move out of the way."

"Begin!" Brenadeir shouted.

The horn sounded.

Darlene turned her gun on Richie.

Richie lifted his sword.

Shelly ducked.

Darlene's hand went left ...

Richie's hand went right ...

When they met in the middle, the blade cut into Darlene's wrist.

21

G unfire blasted Richie's eardrums. Arnold was taking the spray-and-pray approach, waving his Uzi around like a water sprinkler spitting fire. He didn't seem to care how quickly he was churning through rounds. But he managed to land a bullet into every last one of the Red Demons.

Some faltered. Some fell.

"Keep the blood on this side!" Oliver yelled.

"Stop shooting, you idiot! You got 'em!" Wade nudged the Uzi, and the stout man stopped firing.

Darlene wailed, holding a wrist that was cut at the joint, her hand dangling on whatever bundle of ligaments and skin were shredded by the broadsword.

Shelly grabbed Darlene's gun off the floor. "Same team, bitch." She pierced Darlene's foot with the katana, driving it through the grated floor.

Darlene shrieked in agony. "You bitch!"

Shelly and Richie locked eyes. Shelly knew as well as Richie did that Darlene was a liability. And their side needed blood.

Win-win.

"Uh ..." Wade said. "They're not dead."

The Red Demons stumbled, oozing black liquid from their wounds and waddling like drunks.

"Can they not die?" Wade asked.

"Don't let them take you," Arnold commanded.

"Take me where?"

The Red Demons, resurrected, pursued them again, taking small steps and sniffing like zombies powered by smell.

Richie stepped forward. It was time to take control. "Arnold! You don't have a lot of shots left. Stand back here and guard Darlene. She dies, we all lose. And try not to fucking shoot us."

Darlene shouted, "You son of a—"

Shelly caved in the bridge of Darlene's nose with the barrel of the gun, shutting her up.

"Arnold! Get back here!" Richie commanded again.

Arnold scampered toward Darlene. "I'm gonna make you rich, kid," he said to Richie.

The Red Demons shrieked.

Richie looked down the line: Shelly with a 9mm, Wade with sais, Oliver with a battle axe.

Richie nodded. His body drowned in adrenaline, eyes wide, heart drumming like a heavy metal instrumental beat—*drumming, drumming, drumming*. They all nodded back.

Richie drew breath. "Let's go." A battle cry rang from deep within his gut, and when he sprinted forward, the others did as well, marching into the line of teeth and claws before them.

Two Red Demons darted toward Wade.

"Oh fuck!" Wade screamed, skidding against the metal grate and extending his sais.

Shelly squared up and fired a round into each of the beasts, looking like she'd done it before. But the shots did little to deter the snarling, shrieking masses of wide eyes, yellow fangs, and dried skin.

Richie's feet brought him to a cluster of three stumbling Red Demons, wavering over the threshold of the midline between their side and his and sniffing the air. He slowed, gripping his swords, hesitating. It seemed too easy to strike these things down. In their current state, they appeared more like toddlers than monsters.

"Stay back!" Arnold yelled from behind him. A chain of automatic gunfire followed, landing on two creatures that had breached Richie's line.

The beasts in front of Richie all locked their gazes on Arnold as if triggered by the commotion. They emitted a collective screech, opened their jaws wide, and revealed blackened gums underneath.

Richie swung, burying the blade into the neck of one. It swiped at Richie, taking a chunk of skin from his chest.

The other Red Demons rushed forward, barreling toward Richie. He fell backward, keeping his hands on the sword. With the blade stuck in his opponent's neck, he brought the thing down with him. Black blood oozed from its neck, splattering Richie's cheek.

The thing clutched the blade, trying to remove it from its neck, oblivious to the sword's damage to its hands. Richie planted his heel in the thing's rib, and together they rotated, conjoined by the bloodied metal.

Richie climbed to his feet, ripped the sword free, and sent one swift blow down to the Red Demon's neck, ripping through the remaining flesh and cutting straight through to the metal flooring. Black blood sputtered out of the opening, seeping down the grating and filling the reservoir beneath them.

Richie peered up at the clock.

Almost two minutes remained.

An angry scream drew his attention over to Shelly, who dropped the 9mm and held her bleeding bicep. A Red Demon crouched in front of her, ready to pounce.

With two quick strides, Richie jabbed the blade into the creature's jaw, stopping its movement.

The Red Demon's pale eyes turned to him. Richie yanked the blade free, removing the creature's jawbone with it. The Red Demon's black tongue dropped down to its collarbone in a ropey waterfall of blood.

Shelly reached down for the gun with her one useful hand, placed the barrel on the thing's forehead, and shot.

It dropped dead.

Another monster ran through Richie and Shelly, nicking a shoulder each and plowing them over.

Suddenly, the gunshots from the Uzi stopped.

Arnold uttered, "Shit."

Richie looked back. Four red nude bodies lay dead at the feet of Arnold. He turned the Uzi over to use it as a bat as two more approached slowly.

"Help me!" Arnold screamed, his eyes falling on Richie, then Shelly, then Oliver, then Wade.

Behind him, Darlene gripped the handle of the katana that held her foot in place. "Useless." She ripped it out with a squelch of flesh, and instead of a scream, a shrill grumble escaped her throat. She pushed Arnold aside and held the katana high, ready to slice through her attackers.

Wade was on his back, digging his sais into a Red Demon as it swiped at his face, bringing streaks of blood upward.

"Get off me!" Oliver bucked his legs and arms, trying to wiggle free of a group of five Red Demons as he was dragged past the threshold, over to the opposing side.

Another swipe, and a claw caught Wade's cheek wound, pulling the stitches and taking a chunk of skin, leaving two disconnected flaps. He grabbed his face, gurgling on blood as the Red Demon dug its nails into Wade's shoulder and dragged him backward.

Toward the shimmer.

"They're not trying to kill us," Richie said. "They're trying to take us."

"No!" Arnold screamed as the Red Demons converged. Darlene swatted at them, slicing fingers, piercing flesh, until the blade was ripped out of her hand.

"Help those rich assholes," Richie said, holding the broadsword out to Shelly. She took it as he looked over at a screaming Wade being dragged past the open armory. The remaining untouched weapons called to him.

"What the hell are *you* gonna do?" Shelly asked.

They're weaker than they look, Richie thought as he bounded toward the armory, eyes locked in on something shiny, bulky, and powerful.

A chainsaw.

22

R ichie lifted the chainsaw off the notches and cranked the pull cord.

Once ...

Twice ...

On the third pull, it came alive, revving, growling like a starved animal.

Richie glanced back at Shelly as she dodged a claw, then swung down on a Red Demon's skull, catapulting bits of viscera and black brain matter. Darlene finished the thing off by piercing through its neck sideways, then yanking the blade straight through the front of its neck. Shelly ducked as chunks of throat flew past her head.

Richie would be able to take in the absurdity of it all in ...

One minute.

"Richie!" Wade shouted.

Wade was almost through the glimmering veil, every limb subdued by the howling creatures.

Richie and Oliver would need to take them out together.

Richie ran forward to the black side, one hand squeezing the trigger, one hand on the top handle, blade concentrated on the Red Demon dragging Wade backward. Richie was fully aware that what he was about to do would tip the scales in the wrong direction. He hoped there was enough blood on his team's side as he rammed the chainsaw into the Red Demon's mouth. The chainsaw teeth ate through skull and tongue and gums on its way out the back of the Red Demon's head. The chain circulated, flicking skin and flesh into Richie's eyes, slapping his mouth, pouring down onto Wade's face.

Richie pulled the chainsaw upward, splitting the thing's head into two halves.

It released Wade and collapsed.

Panting and holding his shoulder, Wade said, "Goddamn, Richie."

Richie wiped his eyes clean. "We need to help Oliver." He revved the chainsaw again and sprinted.

He aimed the chainsaw blade into the closest Red Demon—the one with Oliver's left foot tucked under its arm—and knifed the chainsaw blade into its back. He lifted it off the ground as its body jerked on the twisting blade.

With his leg free, Oliver whipped his foot around like a kickboxer, freeing his other leg. He got his feet under him with two Red Demons holding an arm each.

Wade sprang into action, running toward the Red Demon holding Oliver's right arm and stabbing him in the forehead with a sai. The thin blade came out as easily as it had entered, and he stabbed again and again.

Oliver threw the remaining grappler to the ground and stomped. The Red Demon's cranium caved with little resistance, cratering like a rotted pumpkin.

"Yeah, bitch!" Wade yelled.

Thirty seconds.

"A little help?!" Shelly yelled, swinging her sword like a torch on the other end of the arena, slashing through the back of a Red Demon. It wasn't enough to stop it from tossing Arnold forward. He landed on his face, busting his forehead on the flooring.

"We need to get back to our side now." Richie backed away from the veil.

A roar erupted. This time it wasn't the crowd. It wasn't a plea for help or a battle cry. It wasn't a squeal from one of those *things*. It was something big. A roar that conjured images of the dinosaurs Richie was afraid of when he was a child.

It came from the other side of the veil.

Richie turned to run.

Something burst through the veil in a flash of red skin and dug its claw into Wade's calf.

It loomed over them, halfway out of the portal. A seven-foot-tall, bright-skinned demon with an extended jaw and a snarling, long snout.

It pulled Wade backward.

Wade stabbed the grated flooring with his sai, stopping his backward slide, but the claws ripped through his leg.

Richie cranked the chainsaw again, bringing it down on the hellspawn's arm.

The beast's other arm appeared through the portal, sending a punch to Richie's chest that lifted him off his feet.

His head hit the ground, dazing him.

He looked up, and through his blurred vision he saw the giant swipe a gash across Oliver's midsection. Oliver rolled to the ground, grabbing his stomach.

Richie tried to shake off the dizzy spell, tried to rattle off his double vision. As he came to his elbows, he knew this might be the end of Wade.

Suddenly, the creature fell forward, stumbling in front of Richie.

Richie summoned his wits and his strength and grabbed the chainsaw at his side.

He lifted the blade in the air.

Activated it.

The creature fell on top of Richie, and the chainsaw spun through its chest. It spat that monstrous howl and a shitload of blood into Richie's face as the life drained out its body.

Rumrumrumrumrumrum!

By the time the horn sounded, Richie was wearing a full coat of the thing's insides.

Richie never thought he'd be happy to hear Brenadeir's voice.

"That's the end of the round! Close the gate!"

Machine gun fire rained down on the Red Demons that remained standing. The elites plugged their ears as suited men standing in the rafters above them cleared the area until only the human contestants remained.

As shell casings and bodies fell atop the platform Richie lay on, he rolled out from under the lifeless hellspawn and looked up at the veil, curious as to what could have forced the beast in his direction.

Only for a moment, the lines of a face and body, lined with scrapes and wet with blood, were visible through the shimmer.

It was Tyler.

Foreign arms wrapped around Tyler's body and pulled him back through. He was there and gone so quickly, Richie questioned whether he'd seen Tyler at all.

When Wade turned to Richie, the look they shared confirmed it.

The power from the control panel shut off in a fading hum.

The light of the symbols went dim.

The veil within the stone-lined frame vanished.

23

"What a show!" Brenadeir shouted. The bulletproof glass slid down from the rafters. "Time to calculate the blood totals."

The screen hanging from the ceiling displayed a jumble of shifting numbers—one side indicating black, one side indicating white.

Richie rose to his feet and screamed over the crowd noise. "Hey! Brenadeir! Was that Tyler!"

His voice couldn't make it to Brenadeir. He wiped the black sludge off his face and shuffled over to Wade.

Wade grunted. "My leg, man. It's—it's fucked."

Richie wrapped Wade's arm around his neck and helped lift the injured man. Wade grunted through gritted teeth.

"What was Tyler doin' in there, man?" Wade asked. "You think Vince is in there too?

"I don't know."

Oliver swooped in and grabbed Wade's free arm. A line of blood had formed across Oliver's stomach, and Richie wondered how deeply he'd been cut.

"You okay?" Richie asked Oliver.

Oliver grimaced and said, "Just a scrape. Stings, that's all."

"That fat asshole was right," Wade said. "We're not leaving this place."

Oliver said nothing.

"We're all getting out of here," Richie said as they walked in a group back to Shelly, Arnold, and Darlene. The three of them were scraped up, bruised, and bloodied, but alive. Richie took just the slightest amount of glee in seeing Darline holding her bloody foot.

"Those two knew what we were walking into. They all did," Wade said. "Those sharks offered us up to those things on a silver platter."

Rage boiled inside of Richie. All he could think of was the soft muscle tissue that comprised Aiden Prince's throat and how easy it would be to crush it.

"I'm gonna kill them," Wade said. "Fuck the rules."

Though Richie didn't say it, he was in a fuck-the-rules kind of mood as well.

The digital display stopped flashing.

"Oh no," Brenadeir said into the microphone. "It appears the black side has won, no doubt, thanks to the violent theatrics of Mr. Richie Stull and his chainsaw."

They closed in on the other half of their group. Wade eased off of Richie's and Oliver's backs and grimaced as he attempted to stand.

"Way to go, Mr. Richie Stull," Darlene said from the floor. "We lost because of you."

Wade shot down to the ground, grabbed Darlene by her blouse, and pulled her in. "Richie saved my life. I would've been taken back into that damn Stonehenge portal twice if it wasn't for him."

"No physical altercations between rounds!" Brenadeir commanded.

Wade released Darlene's blouse, and the shocked look on her face faded. "You're scared," she said. "You should be."

"Now it's time to select who will move on to the next round ... and who will not," Brenadeir said.

Darlene giggled maniacally. "We're all going to hell."

"Mr. Jackson Dawkins, please come forth and pick your champions." Brenadeir removed the microphone from his mouth and waved for Jackson to join him.

Jackson sauntered forward sheepishly, stepping into the light once again with that same dead-eyed expression. The look became clear to Richie, knowing what he knew now—what Jackson knew before they'd started round three. Jackson had faced the monsters. He'd survived the games. Had he watched as his fellow combatants were sacrificed to the things that dwelled on the other side of the portal? There was no hope left in his expression. No light. Only darkness.

Jackson took the microphone and lowered it to his mouth. The crowd went silent, waiting for him to speak.

"Good evening, everyone," Jackson said finally. He spoke slowly, with a faint Southern drawl. "I hope you're enjoying the show. I truly hope you're enjoying the thrills of seeing these people fight for your entertainment. Much like them, I was brought here on the pretense of having my life changed. And, holy shit, was it changed. I'm rich. I'm so rich that the money I have locked away will *make* money that I'll lock away, and on and on in perpetuity." Jackson looked down at the contestants. "And what did it cost me?"

Brenadeir hovered toward him, whispering some version of "stick to the script."

"I've been tasked with picking the champions for this round, but first, I want to talk about my life before this. Brenadeir described me as an activist and an eco-terrorist. I suppose that's fair. The very people in this room are the types that I fought against in my activist efforts. That is, until I realized that no amount of organizing and protesting and begging and appealing to human decency would ever move the needle. No amount of governmental policies can fix a system that's intentionally built to oppress by the very people who implement the policies. So I took more drastic measures. I did things that were unlawful, much like all of you take unlawful actions daily to enrich yourselves. When the government found out I was making a bomb, I was charged with three counts of conspiracy, among other crimes. Brenadeir pulled some strings and saved me from the fate of incarceration so that I could come here and entertain you all on one fateful night."

Jackson cleared his throat. "Here's the thing, though. I now have God-level wealth, which gives me access to resources that most people don't even know about. Like, for instance, explosives that are undetectable to scanners. That and a lot of free time means I've been able to think a lot about what I'm going to do here tonight. You want me to pick a champion? There are none." He looked down at the contestants again. "I'm sorry ... This is for the best."

Jackson released the microphone, then ripped the ends of his shirt, revealing a vest underneath. He removed a device with a wire connected to it from the side of the vest.

The crowd let out a collective gasp.

"Guards!" Brenadeir shouted, backpedaling.

The moment just before the gunfire was eerily calm and quiet, one second stretched to an eternity as Richie processed what was about to happen.

Helena's voice whispered in his ear, *Run.*

Jackson planted a foot on the railing of the suite. Bullets ripped through his skin as he went airborne, diving toward the metal gate and the stones that lined it.

Brenadeir screamed, "NOOOOO!"

Time slowed as Jackson went down ...

But Richie had already turned. He was already sprinting for the waiting room doors.

He'd laid his palm on the stone handle and pulled by the time Jackson popped like a sledgehammer hitting a watermelon. He couldn't see Jackson's body turn to fiery, fleshy confetti, but he did feel the shockwave as it carried him into the waiting room uncontrollably. His knees and elbows rammed against the flooring, and then his forehead. Dazed again, he struggled to lift his head, his brain having slid to and fro like putty in a jar.

The explosion hadn't been as loud as he'd expected, but the screams from the arena were like nails grinding in his ears, amplified by the coma his subconscious threatened to slip into.

A demonic roar overpowered the screams, and he could only assume the gates of hell had truly, in a very real sense, been unleashed.

He wanted to look back, but even if he could, even if he were able to regain enough strength, he wouldn't look back at the damage or what had been released in the wake of it. He couldn't bear the thought of the others dead. Especially Shelly, and even Wade.

Something heavy fell against his leg, and his ankle protested, nearly twisting under the weight.

Finally, Richie regained full consciousness and looked back in time to see Arnold being dragged away, the man's pudgy arms slapping the ground, until a meat hook entered the front of his shoulder and exited the back. What pulled him up on the other side of the hook wasn't one of the emaciated Red Demons Richie had just shredded. This was something bulky and shimmering. Over six feet tall. Skinless. Wet with blood. All of its skin, gone.

It lifted Arnold, the pathetic, whimpering mess, to his feet. With its free hand, the skinless thing grabbed Arnold's jaw, forced his mouth open, and sniffed.

Under the frame of the waiting room doors, the skinless man let out a satisfied, sensuous breath, as if aroused.

Fuck this. Richie pulled himself up, darted toward the elevator door, and tapped the side button again and again and again as if the faster he pressed, the faster it would open. And it couldn't come fast enough. Either the elevator would arrive first, or the chaos that awaited him around the corner would make good on its threat to swallow him whole.

Beyond Arnold's cries, the screams of fear from the arena turned to screams of pain.

The elevator opened.

Richie leapt inside and pressed the button to the first floor.

24

Richie was back in the hall of statues. His unwanted status as a gladiator made more sense now, and he wondered if the statues were a tongue-in-cheek nod to the guests they brought in of what was to come.

All of this was a game to these people.

It was all for fun.

What fun they were having now.

At the end of the hall, a collection of pearls spilled like marbles on the floor, and an elderly woman fell to the ground.

"Martha!" A man who matched the woman's age bent down to help her up.

Until the jagged nails of a red hand clawed at his spine.

The man shouted and fell on top of the woman, his body limp, useless.

A chorus of screams echoed from the banquet hall. The Red Demons had poured out of the arena and into the mansion.

The one Richie was eyeing now moved quicker than what Richie had seen previously. It grabbed the man's head with fervor and twisted it backward with a crunch so that the man's eyes were facing the ceiling. A crackle of death sounded in the man's throat as the Red Demon bent and sniffed.

What the fuck what the fuck what the fuck—it repeated in Richie's head, and for a very brief moment he pondered just what the hell all of these things were smelling for. Some kind of life force a la that cheesy Stephen King movie Richie had seen on cable as a kid?

Richie rewound back through his memory of the night's events before he'd ever gone down the elevator, before he'd stepped foot into this very room, tracking the path back to the front door. He'd have to go through the Red Demon to get there, maybe a few of them. Maybe even step over the man with the crooked neck and his crying partner pinned underneath him on the way. The black blood was still fresh on Richie's skin, still soaked deep into the fabric of his clothing. The pungent smell of metal seeped into his nostrils, reminding him of the things he'd done in the ring. Somehow, as he watched the old woman stuck in place, gasping and reaching for life, swiping the pearls that had fallen from her neck, the dread of it all settled in. Despite what Richie had done in the ring, not helping felt more cruel. But she'd watched him. She'd cheered him on. Had she howled for each death, each scar, each drop of blood?

Richie ran forward, hurtling toward the other end of the corridor, toward the opening where the Red Demon removed the old man's jawbone from the rest of his skull in an attempt to breathe him in. The old woman held up a hand, signaling for help in lieu of breath. The combined weight of the old man and Red Demon was sure to cut off her oxygen soon enough.

A series of images flashed in Richie's mind as he allowed himself the briefest reprieve from the madness.

Richie thought of hanging his jacket on the coat rack after a long day of work.

He thought of Kate's embrace, the way she fit inside his arms so perfectly.

The image of a newborn, dirty and screaming as it was introduced to the sights and sounds of the world.

And he realized the only way he would live those moments was by leaving everyone behind, even the old woman. Even as she attempted to catch both her last clouds of oxygen and Richie's hand.

The Red Demon paid him no attention as Richie ran past the pile it hovered above.

Richie put the old woman and her backwards-facing husband in his rearview. He had to get out. For Kate. For his child.

Four partygoers ran down the staircase, and a swarm of Red Demons followed, leaping and knocking them down the steps in a clumsy series of cracks and squelches and screams. The Red Demons were looking for something, and whatever that something was, it seemed to be hidden in the mouths of Brenadeir's elite class.

A shotgun blast sounded.

Richie looked up to the top of the staircase, where Aiden stood with a twelve-gauge pressed into his shoulder. He pumped it, readying another shot as a slayed demon tumbled down the stairs.

Aiden's eyes found his sponsee. "Richie!" he shouted.

In a moment of paralysis, Richie wasn't sure if he could trust the man who'd led him to this place. This was the same man who promised him prosperity at the expense of a good show and a little violence. But he'd been through the games before and had come out on the other side this beacon of success. He seemed to want the best for Richie, didn't he?

No.

The games had gone tits up. Richie couldn't trust a soul.

"Richie, wait!" Aiden yelled.

Richie ran past the stairwell, making his way back to the front door.

"Richie! The entire place is on lockdown! You won't be able to leave without my help! I can get us out of here!" Aiden climbed down the steps, leaping down the final set of four.

Richie turned, still unsure if he could trust the man, but quickly leaning on the side of *yes.*

"Richie, I'm sorry," Aiden said. "This is so fucked. None of this was supposed to happen this way. You go." He pointed over Richie's shoulder, angling toward the front entrance. "I'll cover us."

A second after Richie turned to make a run for it, he felt a prick on the side of his neck. He winced, his hand shooting toward the pain instinctively.

A syringe clattered on the marble flooring, having fallen from the open hand of Aiden.

"What did you—" A sudden weightlessness overcame Richie. Everything sank like smoked meat peeling off a bone. With his legs unable to keep him upright, Richie collapsed.

Aiden let the twelve-gauge dangle from his shoulder strap, grabbed Richie's blood-soaked collar, and dragged.

He was going the wrong way.
He was taking Richie back to the elevator.

25

"It's a temporary paralyzing agent," Aiden said as the ceiling slid past his head in Richie's vision. "It only lasts about five minutes."

The statues appeared again, and Richie knew it would only be a matter of time before he was back on the elevator.

"I really am sorry," Aiden said. "We get eight contestants. They require six. Why six? Fuck if I know. I didn't make the rules. This was just the agreement. If we don't give them six living bodies, they get angry. When they get angry, they don't give us what we want." He pulled Richie into the elevator. The doors closed, and for a moment, the screams from the mansion subsided.

"You can think we're evil. Just know that we do all of this to create a better future. Your child will have a better future because of what we do here. Because of the People of the Red Night. There's never been prosperity without sacrifice."

Richie tried to speak, but his jaw wouldn't move. All that came out was a measly little moan.

"Don't fight it," Aiden said. "You'll just torture yourself."

The elevator slowed its descent. The door slid open.

"Shit!" Aiden dropped Richie, gripped the shotgun, and fired.

Richie's eardrums cracked in protest, pulsating in agony, begging for cover.

"Good thing these fuckers go down easy." Aiden let the shotgun go slack and dragged Richie by the collar again.

Richie grunted. His jaw moved an inch. His tongue touched the roof of his mouth. The sound that came out was, "Yuh ... Yuh ..."

"Come on, Richie," Aiden said as he pulled Richie out of the waiting room and back into the arena, where warped screams floated around his periphery. "Don't make this harder than it needs to be." He kept a steady hand on the shotgun, eyes darting, head on a swivel.

"Yuh ... You," Richie muttered, using every ounce of energy he had within him to *move, move, move.* "You ... n'ver ... played the ... games ... c'ward ..."

Aiden stopped pulling for a moment, looking down at Richie. His eyes shot upward, and he drew the shotgun once more.

CHK-CHK-BOOM!

"Tell them to stay back!" Aiden yelled. "I'm bringing you an offering! This makes six! Everyone's accounted for!"

A horn blasted, that same damn horn that had called Richie back for each round, and he began to feel it wasn't Brenadeir or any of his goons sounding it. He considered that it might be coming from the other side of that damn gate.

As a rustle of feet and claws tapped against sand and metal, a gaggle of Red Demons ran past them toward the other end of the arena. Richie forced his head to tilt to see what they were running toward. The motion turned his world upside down, which was fitting, because even a right-side-up view would make him feel like he'd gone full tilt crazy.

Standing in front of the portal—the shimmer now a crooked mess resembling a glowing, shattered mirror—was a group of five figures, all sexless, all devoid of skin, and shimmering with wet, pink muscle tissue. As Richie was unwillingly pulled closer, the humanoid creatures became more clear. Some were nearly skeletal, with chunks of flesh missing from their frame, creating an asymmetrical and horrifying appearance.

The Skinless Ones, Richie thought.

One let in a dramatic inhale. "This one does not smell of despair."

Brenadeir's voice sounded from the speaker system. He was still perched on his platform, shielded from the chaos. "I assure you, my friends, he's as desperate as they come. All of our blood bags are."

"Nuh ... Nnnnoooooo," Richie grumbled.

Then another skinless creature said, "We accept."

A third looked up at Brenadeir. A tendon wiggled off its jaw as it spoke. "And you will repair the gate before the next harvest?"

"Absolutely," Brenadeir said into the microphone. "We aim to continue our allyship."

"As do we," the Skinless Ones all said in unison.

They turned and walked back toward the shimmer. One said, "Let's have our dogs fetch the fighters. Toy with them. Have them delivered to us nice and ripe." They disappeared into the shimmer, stepping under the crooked metal frame covered with the thick, wet remains of Jackson Dawkins.

Richie's feet began to tense, but he knew he wouldn't be able to make his legs move in time to escape his fate. He could only watch the portal grow larger as he came closer to it.

"You're a good kid, Richie. Really. And what you're doing now is going to help so many people. You don't know it now, and you may not ever realize it. I want to say thank you. My heart goes out to you." Aiden stopped just inches in front of the portal, regaining his breath. "And no, I didn't play these games. I'm sorry about the little white lie, but ... why the fuck would I do that?"

He grabbed Richie with both hands and heaved.

Then everything was white.

26

Whimpering. Whining. Wailing.

It sounded like an animal being skinned alive, delivered in an otherworldly, pulsing reverberation.

Then, sniffing.

Sharp fingernails climbed into Richie's mouth.

The world came into focus, and all he could see were wide, red, saucer-like eyes staring back at him.

The Red Demon recoiled above him, placing a hand on its nose, coughing.

Richie made a fist.

Shook his arm.

He could move again.

He grabbed the side of the Red Demon's face and threw it to the ground. One punch kept the thing in place. A second punch caved in its skull.

They were scary as shit before he realized how damn flimsy they were. Their skin was like wrapping paper, and their bones were like cardboard.

Hues of red splashed against a starless night sky, with black ash swirling around Richie's vision. The landscape around him conjured images of the aftermath of a wildfire. Dried and cracked dirt. Mounds covered in soot. All the while, a red and yellow glow haloed a perimeter that stretched farther than he could see, and the distance between Richie and that phantom perimeter was lined with spikes and pillars, poles with meat hooks hanging from them, all with bodies entangled on the darkened wood, dried and stained with blood, like a system of telephone poles connected by death.

Richie breathed in ash and coughed it out. The wailing continued, echoing in a way that made it impossible to discern the direction from which it was coming.

Richie stood, his eyes fixed on a naked body parallel to the ground, hoisted up by a series of wooden spikes jutting through its stomach, chest, and one exiting its open jaw. Frightened and certain he was dreaming, Richie approached the body, realizing that the man's eyes were wide open.

His chest was rising up and down, sloshing against the wooden spike.

His eyes shifted to Richie.

Richie leapt backward, his skin raised, blood boiling with fear. His subconscious screamed at him, telling him to run. But there was nowhere to go. Nowhere was safe in this place.

He'd gone to hell.

"No, please!" Richie heard from his periphery. After more rounds of frantic no's and please's, it became clear who the whimpers belonged to.

Arnold Swanson was shrieking in terror.

Richie ran through the rocky terrain that sloped up and down on hard dunes.

"Please!" Arnold shouted again, his voice peaking above a hill in front of Richie.

Richie's hands slapped dried dirt as he climbed the hill, peering above it.

Arnold was on his knees, his clothing ripped clean off, naked as the day he was born. A swarm of Red Demons surrounded him, two holding his arms out straight, crucifixion style. Four others stood in front of him, bobbing slowly back and forth.

Blood trickled down Arnold's bare skin. "H–help! Is anyone there?! Richie?! Wade?! Oliver?! They're killing m—"

Arnold was stifled by his own scream when a Red Demon inserted its bony index finger into his eye socket, turning his eyeball into white and red jelly.

Richie put his feet under him and considered whether he should jump in and save what was left of Arnold, thinking back on Arnold's offer of rewarding Richie for keeping him safe. By that standard, though, Richie had already failed.

But the other, more cynical, half of Richie watched in morbid neutrality, remembering the deception of the games. Remembering what Arnold had knowingly led Richie and the others into.

He would have thought no one deserved to die the way he was witnessing now. But maybe ... just maybe ...

Arnold did.

Another harsh shriek brought Richie back down to whatever earth this place constituted. He remembered the old woman with the scattered pearl necklace, how she reached out for him and would have begged for help if she had the oxygen to speak.

He couldn't leave Arnold here.

Because he wasn't like Arnold.

He began to rise—

And a small, calloused hand slapped against his mouth.

A familiar voice calmed his nerves. "*Shh*. It's me. It's Shelly."

Richie eased up. He watched as the Red Demon wiggled its finger around in Arnold's eyes as if churning butter.

"You go out there and you'll die," Shelly said. "There's nothing we can do to help him."

"What the hell is going on?" Richie asked. "How long have we been here?"

"I don't know. I have no idea what the fuck is going on. I don't know how we all got scattered. I've been looking for Wade and Oliver. All I've found so far is you."

The Red Demon's finger was deep inside Arnold's socket, down to its knuckle.

"We can't just sit here," Richie said. "They're torturing him."

"No, no, they're draining him of something," Shelly said.

"What?

"Just wait."

Though no part of Richie wanted to see what happened next, he did as he was told. Arnold had stopped screaming and begun convulsing.

He's dying, Richie thought as Arnold's round body jerked, jerked, jerked.

Then, the man vomited something black and thick and gelatinous, bubbling and falling from his mouth like raw beef from a meat grinder.

PLOP…

PLOP…

PLOP…

The Red Demons pounced on the liquid in a frenzy, scooping and lapping it up, smearing their faces like hungry wolves.Richie's wide eyes burned as he kept them transfixed on the scene.

When Arnold was done vomiting, he screamed again.

Richie looked at Shelly, who stared back, sharing his wide-eyed expression.

27

"Let's go," Shelly whispered. "We need to find Wade and Oliver."

"We're seriously gonna leave that guy here?" Richie asked.

"You wanna have a bleeding heart here? Be my guest. I'm not ending up like him. And he sure as shit wouldn't come to *your* rescue."

What Shelly hadn't said was the most obvious reason they should leave Arnold behind: Even if he wasn't down one eye and bleeding out, he would still slow them down.

Richie had to go.

Shelly put a hand on his shoulder and squeezed. "Don't you dare feel sorry for that man."

She pulled him, leading Richie down the hill.

"I don't think they're tracking me," Shelly said, "so as long as we stay quiet, we shouldn't draw their attention."

"It seems like they're attracted to smell," Richie said. "Why aren't they coming after us?"

"I don't know, but them *not* attacking us isn't my biggest concern right now." She gained her footing at the bottom of the hill and reached into her pocket. "This is." She pulled out a grey stone, smooth with a symbol engraved on it. "After that Jackson guy kamakaze'd on the gate, I came to beside a couple of these things."

When Richie had last seen the stone, it was on a metal fixture and the hieroglyph had been glowing green. The series of events that preceded this very moment, everything that had gone from bad to worse, seemed to go back to these stones.

"He blew up the gate," Richie said. "I saw it before I was thrown in here. Are you thinking we're going to use those magic stones to get out of here? A bunch of 'em are still on the frame, and we don't even know how they work."

"I don't know what to think, Richie! I just know I don't want to be here!"

"I saw these big, bloody motherfuckers before Aiden tossed me in here ..." Richie's mind trailed off. *Aiden.* A man so shameless he'd lie to make Richie think participating in the games was safe while knowing that Richie was being sent to his death.

"You mean like those emaciated things you chainsawed? Or ... that big motherfucker you chainsawed?"

"They were pretty big. They could talk. I think they ..." *Crazy talk,* Richie thought. *Absolute nonsense.* But he had to get the words out. "I think they have some kind of deal with Brenadeir and his rich friends—"

"Riiiichiiiieee ..."

They both whipped their heads in the direction of a wheezing, breathy whine.

"Shhheeellllyyyy."

"What is that?" Shelly whispered. "Wade? Oliver?"

Richie looked back in the direction from which he'd come, the path he'd stumbled onto before he heard Arnold begging for mercy. The silhouette of that naked man with the three stakes plunged through his body raised its hand.

Richie and Shelly gave each other a puzzled look.

"Hhheeeeerrrreeee," the figure wheezed again.

With Shelly trailing closely behind, Richie walked toward the figure cautiously, the details in its body becoming clear against the backdrop of a hellish orange landscape. The skin was charred to a jerky-like brown, with deep cuts lining its skin like a maze. What little hair was left on the scalp dangled downward, bobbing up and down as the body writhed against the spikes.

Richie slowed his steps. "Uh ... H–hello?"

The body's eyes darted in his direction. "Rich—" It coughed. "Sorry, it's hard to breathe with this thing in my chest."

Richie stuttered. "Uh–um ..."

"Who the hell are you?" Shelly asked.

"You're not ..." The body wheezed. "... gonna believe this ... It's me ... It's Helena."

Richie shot a glance at Shelly, who was less shaken than he was. If she was considering the same questions that festered in his mind, she didn't show it. Was it actually Helena? Was this a trap? If it *was* a trap, how did this thing know about Helena? Was this place really hell and was it reaching into Richie's mind and feeding off of his guilt? Did it know that he wished he hadn't allowed Helena to end her own life?

"Bullshit," Shelly fired back. "We watched Helena Vanderloo die. What do you want?"

"Well," the body said, "for starters, you could get me off of these spikes."

"How can you be her?" Richie asked.

"Long range," the body said. "It was good advice, wasn't it?"

A long breath escaped Richie's chest. "Holy shit."

"I told you I had a way to beat the game," Helena said. "I just had to be dead first to put the wheels in motion." She laughed.

28

S helly walked off, leaving the bizarre scene behind her.

"Wait!" Richie ran after her, temporarily abandoning the charred, raised body suspended on the stakes. He touched Shelly's shoulder, and she spun around.

"Richie, I don't know where we are, I don't know how we got here, and I don't know what the hell that thing is, but I know it's not Helena," Shelly said.

"I'm gonna tell you something crazy," Richie said. "Shit, if I heard it come out of someone else's mouth, I'd think it's crazy too, but look … Helena's been talking to me. Like … from the other side."

Shelly took a moment, staring at Richie with a confused expression. "Huh?"

"We don't have a lot of time here. We *will* get hunted down. Look, before she stabbed herself, she told me she knew how to beat the game. Ever since … I've been hearing her in my head. Her little episodes she had when she was still with us? I think she was talking to the people who lost the games *before* us."

"All those times you were spinning in circles talking to yourself … Was that her?"

Richie held up his hands in surrender. Because saying "yes" would feel too absurd.

Shelly huffed out a deep breath. "I'm sorry this has all gotten to your head, but I'm done being toyed with. I'm getting out of here. You can come with me or stay with the corpse. I don't give a shit."

"Fine," Richie said. "Like it or not, we all need each other. And Helena's our best chance at leaving this place. I'm going back." He turned.

Shelly grunted in protest. Her footsteps pattered in Richie's direction, all the way to the corpse on the stakes.

Richie raised his hands awkwardly, trying to determine the best maneuver to get the corpse off the spikes.

"Stop," Shelly said.

Richie obeyed.

"So you can talk to the dead, huh?" Shelly asked.

The body wheezed. "Long as I can remember. Trust me when I say I wish I couldn't."

"Both my parents are dead," Shelly said. "Talk to them."

Helena coughed. "It doesn't really work like that."

Shelly shot Richie a look.

"It requires some kind of connection," Helena continued. "The ones who'd fallen in the mansion called to me because *we* were in the arena."

Shelly put a hand on the corpse's stomach. "There, that's your connection. Go ahead. Find my parents in some magical spirit realm."

"Okay." The corpse breathed deeply. "Let me see what I can do." The corpse went silent, its eyes remaining open as its body raised and lowered on the spikes.

Shrieks sounded from over the hill. Arnold again. Richie imagined him being drained bone-dry of whatever liquid was being secreted from his body. Tension rose in Richie's chest as he wondered where the Red Demons would go next once they were done with Arnold. Would they catch his scent and come over that hill?

"Let's just take her down and leave," Richie said.

"Not until I have a reason to trust this," Shelly said. "Come on. Give me something."

Richie kept his gaze on the hill, and instead of the Red Demons, with their snarling fangs and wide eyes, it was Arnold who appeared. Naked, eye socket leaking as he dug his fingers into the ground, catching Richie and Shelly in his sights.

"Shit," Richie said. "Shelly, we gotta go now."

With her hand pressed firmly against the corpse's stomach, Shelly turned her head in Arnold's direction. "Fine." She removed her hand.

Arnold yelped, "Help m—!" A gurgling sound escaped his throat, and that same fatty liquid sprang out with it.

"Your parents," the corpse said. "Oh, they're pissed."

"What?" Shelly asked.

The corpse replied, "You must've had a good reason to kill them."

29

"Quick," Shelly said, "let's get her down."

The Red Demons had begun cresting over the hill, crawling toward Arnold and rubbing their grotesque faces in his bile as he dry heaved.

"Please help!" Arnold yelled. He climbed to his knees, ready to make a beeline toward them.

"Richie," Shelly whisper-shouted, crouching under the corpse. "Come help me push her off."

Together, they pressed the body high off the spikes, with Richie giving the final push up and letting Helena plummet like an old, discarded doll down to the cracked earth. It wasn't as difficult as Richie had expected. The body was all skin and bones, weighing close to seventy pounds, if Richie had to guess.

Helena took in two deep breaths and hinged upright. "That's better."

Arnold ran toward them. A claw pierced his ankle, jutting through tendons and bone, and he screamed. Another geyser of goo spouted from his mouth.

A horn blasted from deep within the red and orange distance. The Red Demons straightened up. The one holding Arnold's ankle dragged him toward the sound of the horn.

"We need to follow him," Helena said through the withered body she inhabited.

"Fuck that," Shelly protested.

Helena ran a finger around the edges of the hole in her chest. "We need to be where they take their prisoners if we have any chance at opening that gate again. Treatise between worlds."

Richie thought back to earlier that night. "That's what Brenadeir told us."

Helena nodded. "We need to find whoever's on the other end of that agreement—"

Richie finished her thought. "And change the terms."

"We have to find Tyler and Wade first," Richie said.

"We're not going on a rescue mission," Shelly responded. "We might as well drop dead here."

The Red Demons dragged Arnold away, and though he was swallowed by the mist, his shouts echoed through the void. As long as he shouted, he'd be easy to track.

"We need to stay close," Helena said. The shell her consciousness inhabited willed itself forward. Its bones cracked, and she grunted as the muscles stretched beyond what their rigid, atrophied state would allow. "God, I didn't think being in a dead guy's body would hurt so much."

Richie watched her go, amazed that the body stayed upright. It appeared that at any moment the bones could collapse like a building at a demolition site. And there was also the matter of three wet gaping holes giving Richie a view straight through her pelvis, stomach, and chest.

"Helena," Shelly said, following slowly by her side, "how are you in this dead guy's body in the first place?"

Richie walked forward as well. "Yeah, it's one thing to be able to commune with the dead. I mean, I've seen mediums on TV and shit, but this ..."

Helena spoke through a hoarse throat and pained movements. "I'm learning all of this myself. There's something different about this place. It's hard to explain. My connection to the dead is so much stronger here. Before, it was like being an infant and learning shapes and colors, but here, it's like I'm fluent in a new language. Maybe because this place is *closer* to death and further from living. My connection to the dead. I never understood it. Never wanted it. But I always hoped I could use it for some kind of good. For a year I've been using it to try to find my father. To find out how he died. To see if it was my mom who did it."

Richie and Shelly shared a glance.

"Yeah, we met her," Richie said. "Doesn't really seem like the doting wife type. She tried to kill me."

"Richie damn near sliced her hand off," Shelly added. "I stabbed her in the foot. Oh, and broke her nose. Sorry."

Helena laughed, then continued, "I think I know why I couldn't find him. Why I couldn't reach my dad in the afterlife. I think he's trapped here in this in-between place. Being tortured."

"Fuck," Shelly whispered.

"Those who survive long enough become those things you saw. The lucky ones die before they turn. Like the guy I'm wearing now." The body raised its hands as it walked. "His name was Jacob Cagnetti, and he was more than happy to lend his body to me."

Even through the grunts, she seemed so calm, so self-assured, that Richie had forgotten she'd died by her own hand.

"So you ..." *Killed yourself*, Richie thought, but words wouldn't come out. "How did you know all of this would happen? That we would end up here?"

"The dead talk," Helena answered. "One contestant died in the last game. Jackson Dawkins promised him—*all* of them—that he'd come back and destroy the gate. Make sure none of this happened."

"Couldn't have given us a heads up?" Richie asked.

"I was having episodes and talking to myself. You wouldn't have believed me."

"I wouldn't have fucking believed any of this," Shelly said. "Whoever we see at the end of this trail ... How bad is it gonna be?"

Helena didn't answer.

"That bad, huh?" Richie asked.

"Someone's close," Helena said. "I think it's ..."

A silhouetted figure stumbled in the distance, rummaging through fog and soot. It collapsed to its knees.

"Oliver," Helena said.

Behind Oliver, a shadow loomed. It wrapped its pointy fingers around Oliver's shoulder and held him upright.

30

Richie rushed toward the haggard Oliver.

As Richie came closer, Oliver's appearance grew clearer, as did that of the thing behind him. A wound that ran diagonally across Oliver's face, leaving his nose a mess of cartilage and skin. His body was riddled with cuts like he'd lost a fight with a badger. He held the side of his stomach, but his hands did little to block his insides from getting out.

He opened his mouth, and blood erupted from it, spurting like a broken faucet.

The thing behind him whimpered, "No, no, no, no, no …" It was similar to the Red Demons Richie had fought, the ones who'd taken Arnold, but one eye was intact, with a darting pupil, and its skin, while a similar shade of red, was less thinned-out. Standing naked, even his manhood remained, unlike the others. Maybe he was degenerating? Maybe he was becoming one of them.

Suddenly aware that he had nothing to fight with, Richie tensed his hands, balling his fingers into fists. "Let him down."

"He can't die," the thing said.

So, it can speak, Richie thought.

Richie stepped forward. "Drop him. Now." The thing didn't relent, but as Richie came closer … closer …

The almost-Red-Demon sniffed … sniffed …

When Richie closed in on ten feet of distance between them, he cranked back his elbow, preparing for a fight.

The thing gagged. "Oh, goddamn you." He dropped Oliver and covered his mouth. "Don't come near me." He hissed as he spoke. A side effect of the degeneration, Richie figured. "He'ssssss dying. If he diessssss, he won't be able to feed usssss. We musssst eat thissss harvessssst."

Shelly walked up behind Richie. "Is that thing ... *afraid* of you?"

"Hell if I know," Richie said, looking over Oliver's head as he bled out and toward the thing behind him. "Hey! What do your people want with us?!"

"We jussssst want to eat," the thing said.

"But you're not eating anyone! So what the fuck does that even mean?" Richie marched forward.

"Oh, god. He's really messed up," Shelly said as they reached Oliver.

"The Old Ones will be devasssstated," the thing said as he backed away.

"Answer me!" Richie yelled. "What do you want?"

The thing turned and ran.

Richie gritted his teeth, then refocused his attention on Oliver. Normally, he'd have more sympathy. The death of Vince was still fresh in his mind, but seeing Oliver ripped to shreds, his skin turned to mulch, overwhelmed Richie with sadness.

Slowly, Oliver peered upward. More blood dribbled from his lips as he spoke. "Mason ... tripped into a spike and busted his brains open trying to get away from those things ... Are we in hell?"

Richie took in his surroundings again, if only to convince himself that he hadn't imagined it all. "Yeah, I think so."

"What the fuck are you guys doing here? I should be here, not you."

Richie and Shelly fell silent. It was hard to argue after they'd seen what he'd done.

"Neither should Wade," Oliver said, his speech slowing. He leaned backward, then steadied himself. "Something took him. It took him and not me. Why would they take him and not me? I deserve all this. None of you do." He coughed. "I didn't wanna kill Vince. I didn't wanna kill him. I didn't think I could do it. Helena's mom ... She said she'd pay me ten million to kill him. And I did it. I killed him. I had to kill him. I hate that I *had* to kill him. I saw that Arnold guy get forced into the game, and it made sense. She wanted him gone. Maybe she rigged this whole thing—forced Brenadeir to change the rules—just to whack Arnold. I don't fuckin' know why. God, rich people are petty."

Helena's new body stepped between Richie and Shelly. "Hi, Oliver."

Oliver squinted, taking in the dried, blackened body, and said, "Whoa."

"Where was Wade taken?" Helena asked. "Give us a direction."

Oliver raised his hand, aiming it toward the same area that Arnold had been dragged off to. "He was blowin' chunks, man. This thick, sloppy stuff. What the fuck is going on? I killed Vince. They should have taken me. Why didn't they take me?" He coughed. "I don't know why I did any of this. I don't want the money anymore." He looked up at the sky. "Look at what the world has taken from people like us. Did you see the way they laughed? The way they cheered when I killed Vince? What kind of world do we live in where people like them cheer for the suffering of people like us?"

A long moment of silence grew between them, three gladiators and a revenant spread across the desert lands of a hellish world. With the panicked surge of adrenaline subsiding, Richie realized how tired his body was, how tender the bruises on his shoulder and arms were, how sore the back of his head was, and how everything inside of his mouth stuck together like superglue.

There was no telling how long they'd last, so they had to move.

"You're about to die, Oliver," Helena said.

A heavy breath left Oliver's lungs. "Yeah ... I think so."

Oliver collapsed, falling forward as his last breath exited his body.

Richie stood still, staring at the backside of the dead man.

Until that horn blasted again.

"It seemed like that thing was *sad* that Oliver was dying," Richie said. "If they want to eat, why didn't they take him? Why do they seem repelled by us?"

"I think I understand now," Helena said. "Why would Brenadeir lure a bunch of poor, desperate people into the Night Games just to ship them off to this place and feed these things?"

Richie and Shelly waited for her to finish.

"Because they *feed* on despair," Helena said.

Richie considered it for a moment. "So, that black goop shit that was coming out of Arnold ..."

"Despair materialized," Helena answered.

Despair. The word writhed in Richie's head like a worm, and the image of the Skinless Ones lined up in front of the twisted frame formed with it. "This one doesn't smell of despair," one of them had said of Richie.

"Fuck," Shelly said. "Who's more desperate than someone who has everything but wants more?"

"Exactly," Helena said excitedly. "Richie, what's your primary emotion right now? Is it despair?"

"No, I–I don't think so," Richie replied.

"I know what it is," Shelly said. "It's rage."

Richie gave her a look and nodded. "Yeah."

"Yeah," Shelly said. "I'm pretty pissed off too."

"Hold onto that feeling," Helena said. "Seems like it's keeping the two of you alive."

Richie stepped forward. "We stash the stones in Oliver's body."

"What, like, shove the stones inside of him? Why?" Shelly asked.

"He's dead. If what Helena's saying is true, then they won't go near him. And the stones might be our only leverage."

"You have the stones?" Helena asked.

"Our only leverage for what?" Shelly asked.

"I saw them talking to Brenadeir before Aiden shoved my ass into the portal. They told him to fix the gate, or they weren't going to hold up their end of the agreement."

"You have the stones that go on the gate?" Helena asked again. "The connection between this world and our world?"

"Only two of them," Shelly clarified.

Helena chuckled through her meat suit. Loose flesh dangled from the hole that lined her body as it shook with laughter.

"What's so funny?" Richie asked.

"My father was under contract with William Brenadeir. He helped build his mansion, and then he built something with so much red tape he couldn't even tell his own daughter. But I heard the arguments between him and my mom. She spoke of what she called unconscionable amounts of knowledge. He spoke of chaos. He wanted to shut it down. I think she conspired to get rid of him because of it. Something so powerful he was put in a lockbox so that he could never speak about it again. Something involving ..." She laughed again. "... stones and a gate."

"Your father *built* the damn thing?" Shelly asked.

"I believe he did," Helena replied.

That small window of hope softened the rocky mess in Richie's gut. Stuck in the pits of hell, he'd take all the hope he could get. "We have the missing stones and, if we can find him, the man who built the gate. The mansion's on full lockdown for the next, what, hour or so? And these things don't realize there's a buffet on the other side of that gate. A feeding frenzy of miserable assholes who will blow chunks here forever knowing that they'll never get to see their possessions again. We just have to convince the things here that they're eating the wrong people. All the desperation housed inside that mansion ... they'll be eating for a lifetime."

31

Richie, Shelly, and the revenant that was Helen walked the hellscape, moving past rotting corpses, bodies bloated, blistered, and frozen in perpetual agony, moving toward the growing chorus of screams.

For Richie, it felt like he was walking toward certain doom. He pushed back thoughts of Kate and the life growing inside of her. It had been what kept him fighting earlier in the night, but now his superpower was the heatwave released in his skin every time he thought of Aiden.

Of Brenadeir.

Of Darlene.

All of the People of the Red Night.

How many people just like Richie, Shelly, Oliver, Wade, and Tyler had they watched fight for scraps, rip each other to pieces, on the false promise of a full belly and a fat bank account? How many people had they watched get shuttled off into the gate, never to return? To become one of these zombies feeding on the despair of the next incoming group of fighters?

Eating each other.

Repeating the cycle.

Over and over again.

Stay there, Richie thought. *Focus on that feeling.*

His whole life, he was told to play by the rules dictated by others. To work hard and get ahead. But, as much as he hated to admit it, Aiden

Prince was right. No amount of hard work could beat a rigged system. One that despises people like him. One that keeps the less fortunate fighting amongst themselves, begging for the ones who govern it to give them scraps.

Violence, Richie thought. The ones who govern do so with violence. Not directly. Much like a cult leader can use his influence to carry out executions in the name of a higher power and never lift a finger. Those who govern build the arena. They force the peasants to fight. They laugh because it entertains them.

Yes, Richie had been told he needed to *fit* into this system of violence. A system of complacency in the face of brutality. He understood now that violence was the only way to dismantle it.

He realized that he was always holding back. He was never meant for polite discourse, for champagne and fancy suits. There had always been a fire of rage burning inside of him.

It was time to let that out.

"Munchausen by proxy." Shelly snapped Richie's attention away from his own thoughts.

"What?" Richie responded.

"My parents were killing me," Shelly continued. "They told me they were taking care of me. When I was a little girl, I was too dumb to know the difference. When you're young, you ask questions. You accept the answers. But then you get older and you start noticing things. Like how your mom never leaves you alone with a physician. Or how your dad never lets you see how he prepares the food you eat, even when you ask to see it. How the meals always taste just a little bit better a week before you're scheduled to do blood work. But a kid can only accept bullshit for so long. Eventually, you push back. When I got smart ... when I pushed back ... they got wise, and all I got was sicker." She paused.

In the silence between them, the eerie swell of screams ahead became more prominent. A thick, red fog clung to the air between them and their destination, but Richie knew they must be getting close. Shelly must have felt it, too. What she was saying sounded like a confession dropped at the feet of God or Jesus or whomever would have greeted them in front of the pearly gates.

Richie said, "Shelly—"

"I killed them. I did it. I've never told anyone that in my entire life. Every Friday night, I'd get drowsy. I'd sleep for ten hours straight. When I found out it was just another drug they were using on me, something to keep me sedate while they got shitfaced and didn't have to deal with me for a night, I figured I'd turn the tables a bit.

"One night, I found the shit they used to make me drowsy, and I snuck it in their liquor. I was worried it was too much. That maybe they'd never wake up. And I realized how much better off I'd be without them. No matter what hell they put me through, anything would be better than living as their puppet. So I set fire to the house." She took a deep breath, reliving the moment again.

"It was ruled an accident, thank god. I never told law enforcement I knew what my parents were doing to me. I played the part of a dumb kid who didn't know she was a victim. If I let on that I knew, they'd slap me with a motive. When I got better, I kept things quiet. I'd lost both of my parents in a fire. Boo-hoo. I had to keep on weeping for them. Weeping for the people who ruined my body, my life, who stole my childhood from me."

Helena placed a slimy, rotted hand on Shelly's shoulder as they walked. To Richie's surprise, Shelly let the moist skin remain on her shoulder.

"I'm so sorry, Shelly," Helena said.

Richie added, "I didn't know my parents very well, but I'd damn sure rather not know them than have to go through any of that."

"I dream about that night sometimes," Shelly said. "Being there, smoke in my face, watching the flames slap at the stars. I've always wondered if they woke up while the house was on fire. If they *knew* they would burn to death and just had to accept it before their brains boiled and the light went out." She turned to Helena. "Do you know?"

Helena nodded. "I do."

The fog lifted, and they slowed at the site of the structure before them. It appeared to be a quarter-mile wide, with bits of bodies stacked on top of each other, congealing into one jagged, castle-like formation. While bits of disembodied bone and flesh lay strewn about the cruel tapestry, some bodies remained intact but in various states of decay. Some of them screamed for help, somehow still alive under the weight of death above them.

Richie's breath shook, the filthy air of the place catching in his throat. "Oh my god." He gazed upon the sight in the same way he might've gazed upon the burning wreckage of a plane crash, so uncanny and unconscionable that his mind couldn't rationalize it.

"Tell me," Shelly said.

"They woke up to the fire," Helena answered. "They knew they would burn to death. And they knew it had to have been you who started the fire."

Shelly exhaled. "I'm glad we got that squared away."

They all stood shoulder-to-shoulder, taking in the pile of corpses that comprised the castle. Straight ahead—twenty feet away—was an opening, and more screams echoed from within.

"Everybody ready?" Richie asked.

"Let's go knock on the fucking door," Shelly answered.

32

If they'd just travelled from the barren outskirts of hell, they were now stepping foot into the epicenter. The stench made Richie gag, and he couldn't tell if it was from the flesh rot or from the blood that had formed a red mass beneath the live bodies sagging by strands of back skin off of meat hooks, taking sad, desperate breaths. Men lay bound on slabs, their chests flayed open, revealing the muscle tissue underneath.

The Red Demons surrounded Richie, Shelly, and Helena, forming a perimeter around them, but keeping their distance.

The screams were unlike anything Richie had heard before. He'd rather listen to a baby scream. He'd rather listen to an animal cry in agony. Anything other than the chorus of pain within the bloody castle.

"Keep it together," Richie instructed Shelly and Helena under his breath, but he just as well needed the encouragement himself.

"Your leaders," Richie said to the starved demons. "Where are they?"

He didn't expect an answer, and the zombies didn't disappoint. They snarled without lips and stared with those giant lidless eyes.

Instead, the answer came from deep within the structure with a scream from a familiar voice: "No! Please!"

"You hear that?" Shelly asked.

"Arnold," Richie replied.

Richie eyed the creatures that surrounded him, then took a step forward.

The circle stepped with him, keeping the radius around them stable.

"We keep moving forward," Shelly said. "We keep our eyes ahead."

"So many people ..." Helena whispered.

"We can't help them," Shelly said.

"She's right," Richie added. "Let's move. All together."

The Red Demons followed like a swarm of bees as Richie attempted to drown out the cries in his periphery and focused in on Arnold's voice. His feet sloshed against the bloody floor, soaking his shoes and socks. They zagged around columns of bones stacked ten feet high, past displays of bodies bound and broken and pretzeled into bizarre tapestries.

They approached a crowd of Red Demons, hundreds of them yelling, gyrating around a circular platform of raw flesh. On top of the platform were Arnold, Wade, and Tyler.

Each was chained to the floor, and the ends of the chains had spikes jutting through their forearms and shins. A sea of black goo surrounded them, with remnants of it hanging from their chins, chests, and shirts. The Skinless Ones that Richie saw standing outside the portal stood behind them now. Six of them, identical, shimmering, moist, and grinning as they poked each of their prisoners with knives and hooks, then smiling in delight at the funnel of black liquid that followed thereafter, showering the frenzied Red Demons.

"Eeeeeeeaaaaat!" the Skinless Ones commanded in unison.

The Skinless Ones were like a hive mind, Richie thought. A shared consciousness finishing the threads of each other's thoughts.

"What do we do?" Shelly asked.

Richie's eyes centered on Tyler, who'd been happy when he last saw him. He'd been smiling, hadn't he? Smiling even though he'd lost. Smiling because he was proud of himself. Richie tried to remember how he looked then, because the scared man on the platform was someone he didn't recognize. Someone who'd been stripped of all hope, had let go of any notions of survival, and now hoped instead for death.

"I–I don't know," Richie said.

"'Ey!" Helena shouted.

All eyes clung to Helena, Richie, and Shelly. There was no silence in a monument of pain, but a still tension hung heavy in the air as every party waited for the next motion.

The Skinless Ones began to speak. "Our other contestants have arr—"

"Shut up," Helena said. "We have a deal to make with you and there's not a lot of time."

She marched toward the platform. Richie and Shelly followed. The crowd split, carving a path for the three of them.

"We know who they are ..." one skinless being said.

"But who are *you*?" another asked.

"Helena Vanderloo," Helena said through the corpse she was wearing. "I died earlier tonight."

"Fascinating," a Skinless One said.

Another Skinless One gagged.

Then another. "What is that stench?"

Helena stopped in front of the platform. "That's us."

Intentionally or not, Helena's moxy empowered Richie. He no longer saw the ones on the platform as monsters. He saw frightened creatures who hoped he wouldn't come closer. Their throats gurgled as they stepped backward, away from Arnold, Tyler, and Wade. The Skinless Ones stayed upright in forced composure, but they looked very, very uncomfortable.

"You came back for me," Arnold said with a glimmer in his one good eye. "I'm gonna make you rich."

"Don't you ever shut the fuck up?" Wade said, breathing puffs of air through his flapping cheek.

"We've come to speak directly to you," Richie said to the Skinless Ones. "You've made a deal with William Brenadeir. We'd like to make a counteroffer. And I really think you'll want to hear it."

One of the Skinless Ones grinned and licked its upper lip. "Vanderloo ... Has the girl come to retrieve her father?" The others laughed. "She might not like what she finds."

Richie sensed Helena tense up. "Stay with us," Richie whispered.

Helena took a deep breath and softened, ignoring the question.

"You rely on William Brenadeir to feed you desperate people, correct?" Richie asked.

"We feed on despair," one said.

"We crave it," another said.

"Yeah, okay," Richie responded. "What I'm trying to understand is, what do you give them in return?"

The Skinless Ones laughed.

One said, "Knowledge."

Another said, "Humans only experience time on a linear plane."

Another said, "Learn from the past."

Another said, "Predict the future."

Another said, "We see all of time. All that has happened. All that will happen."

Another said, "Yet all we crave is despair."

Another said, "To the ones who give us desperate souls, we in return give them … knowledge."

"Arnold," Shelly said to the eyeless, naked man, "you got somethin' to add."

"I'm sorry," Arnold answered, taking a look at Richie, Shelly, Tyler, and Wade individually. "I'm sorry to all of you. I'm sorry to anyone who ends up here, but you have to understand the power that we're dealing with by working with these people. They have something we need but could never have. Endless knowledge. Technologies that haven't been invented yet. Cures for terminal illnesses. Exact dates of recessions. The start of wars. The outcomes of those wars. They know all of this because their brains are unobstructed. They know everything, yet they don't need it. We have the one thing they need. And our world's full of it."

"You disgusting little son of a bitch," Wade said. "You fucking *knew* this would happen to us?"

"Now, now," a Skinless One said. "You'll spoil your innards."

"The gate's damaged," Richie said. "Brenadeir won't be able to fix it, but we will."

Together, the Skinless Ones said, "How?"

"You clearly know who my father is. Bring him to us," Helena said.

33

"My father created the gate. Only he can repair it," Helena said.

"You lie," one of the Skinless Ones said.

"William Brenadeir will restore it," another said.

"We've seen what powers the gate," Shelly fired back. "It's not enough to repair it. It requires the stones. The ones with the glowing symbols. They don't have all of them. When the gate was damaged, some of the stones split. Some of them spilled over into this world."

"We have those missing stones," Richie added. "You have the one person who can put everything back in place. William Brenadeir has nothing you want. You require six bodies for your harvest, is that correct?"

"Yes," the Skinless Ones all said enthusiastically.

"How many do you see before you now?" Richie asked. "Brenadeir has broken the agreement, has he not?"

"He has," one of the Skinless Ones said.

"On the other side of that gate," Richie continued, "is a murderer's row of desperate people. They have everything our world can offer, yet *still* they barter with you because it's not enough. What do you think will happen to someone like that when they realize they'll lose everything?" Richie shot a look at Arnold. Tipped his chin up. "People like him."

A brief moment of silence hung between the parties.

"The veil is fading," one of the Skinless Ones said.

"We presume you have less than an hour remaining in your world's time before it closes," another said.

"With the stones separated, the gate will remain closed for an eternity. We will starve," another said.

"Then let us be your allies," Richie said. "In exchange for our efforts, you free everyone you pulled from the game. Everyone still living. You'll have hundreds in return soon."

"Everyone except this asshole," Shelly pointed at Arnold. "You can have your way with 'im."

"W–what?" Arnold cried. "No. I meant what I said. I'll make you wealthy beyond your wildest damn imagination. Please!"

"No one wants your blood money!" Wade shouted.

"Trust me, you want what I can offer," Arnold shot back.

"None of that matters anymore, sweetheart," Shelly said. "No one's saving you. We sure won't. You're gonna rot here with the rest of your friends."

Arnold burped. Black liquid bubbled out of his throat. He aimed his head downward, and a fountain of ooze spurted from his mouth.

"See?" Richie said. "There are more just like him. They're all on the other side of that thing you call the veil. All on lockdown, sitting on their hands until the moment they can leave. You can have as many as you want."

The Skinless Ones laughed.

One said, "You expect us to oppose them with their weapons?"

"Bullets run out," Shelly said. "And clearly your people out-number them."

"And what of the Great Corruptor?" they said.

Shelly and Richie looked at each other, unsure how to respond.

"The book that keeps us bound here," a Skinless One said.

"Controls us," another said.

"Keeps us locked in this forever contract," another said. "Birthed from the incantations of those who feared us. With the Great Corruptor, William Brenadeir could end our existence. It is why we are in his debt."

What was left of Richie's fractured mind—between the exhaustion, hunger, and dehydration—cycled back through the preceding events of the night, back to the room of ancient trophies when Aiden was displaying William's toys like a luxury car salesman, moving toward the back of the room.

There it what, tucked away in the back of Richie's mind. *The Great Redeemer*, Aiden had called it. That book with brown pages, bound by skin. What was it Aiden had said?

Knowledge comes with consequences. Strings. When you become as powerful as William Brenadeir, the need for contingencies becomes necessary. If you open the floodgates to knowledge, you damn sure better have a back stop.

Richie didn't realize it then. His mind was abuzz with confusion, a desire to leave, and a will to fight for his family all at once. Aiden—simple, hubristic Aiden—was sharing the *backstop*, showing Richie how they'd end the Skinless Ones if they had to.

"Is the cover of this book sewn together with skin?" Richie asked.

"Yes," they all said.

"I've seen it. I know where it is. It's on the fourth floor of Brenadeir's mansion."

"If someone speaks from it," a Skinless One said, "it could be the end of us."

"Then we get there first and take it," Richie said. "Do we have a deal?" His heart skipped a beat when the words came out. Still, he pressed. "If not, we walk out of here and you and your people starve."

One said, "Is the enemy of my enemy ..."

Another said, "My ally?"

Richie didn't hesitate. "Yes."

They all answered, "We accept."

"Then fetch me my father," Helena said. "Now."

"Meet us at the veil," a Skinless One said.

"We shall bring him to you with our army," another said.

"But first," another cut in, "you may choose from our weaponry. We keep what comes through the gate. Anything that might damage the spirit."

They all laughed.

A knot twisted in Richie's gut as he realized what he'd just done. He'd made a deal with devils to kill devils, and he wasn't sure which side was more evil.

But he was sure which side would lose.

"Release the prisoners," a Skinless One said.

They took great pleasure in removing the spikes from everyone on the platform slowly and painfully.

Everyone except Arnold, who begged, pleaded, swore, and prayed to a god that didn't rule over this realm

Tyler cried when he stumbled off the platform and into the arms of Richie and Shelly, showering them with an abundance of thanks. Wade did no such thing. He didn't cry, but Richie knew he was on the cusp of it. The side of his face with the cheek skin hanging off made it look like he was wearing a perpetual smile. Wade didn't say thank you, nor did he need to, but Richie knew he thought it. That might've been enough after what Wade had been through.

When the Skinless Ones brought their prisoners-turned-allies to the weapons display full of battered blades, Richie reached for the double-bitted battle axe, surprised at the light weight and the ease with which he could swing it.

It would have to do.

34

With a broadsword in his hand and a dagger tucked into his belt, Wade limped out of the body castle, refusing help and grinding his teeth with each step. The wounds on his calves were wet, purple, and fresh.

Tyler was less prideful and allowed himself to be propped up by Richie and Shelly, each dragging battle axes in their free hands. Knowing he'd be useless in a fight, Tyler had opted out of picking his weapon. Richie hoped this would all be over for him soon. Over for them all.

The demon swarm followed them all the way back to the opening and then stayed put as they left. Helena walked slowly behind them.

"Is that really Helena?" Tyler asked as they widened the distance between them and the bleeding castle.

"A lot o' shit we can't explain here, man," Richie said. "Long story short: She can speak to the dead and convinced one to give up his body so that she could use it to find her dad."

"Fuck," Tyler said.

"Yeah, that's pretty much what I said, too," Shelly replied.

Tyler sniffled. His voice shook. "I thought I was gonna die."

Wade turned to them and walked backwards. "What do you mean, *thought*? Wake up, big guy. We're dead. Dude exploded, we all died, and here we are."

"I know it seems like we're in hell," Helena said. "But we *will* get out. And you'll need to be in the right state of mind when we get to the other side of the veil."

"Oh, you misunderstand me." Wade turned around and continued speaking with his back facing them. "I fully acknowledge that this is hell. And it's gonna be metal as fuck when we break out of it."

Tyler sucked snot back into his nose. "What are we even going to do when we get there, though? They got guns. They'll shoot all of us on sight."

"They don't know we're coming," Richie said. "How could they? They think they put us in a meat grinder. All except Helena's mom. Guess they chose her as their champion."

"What about Oliver?" Wade said, looking back. "Did anyone see him? I know. We all saw what he did. He's a bastard, but ... he did try to save me, so that's something, I guess."

"He died," Shelly said. "We stashed the stones inside the body so that those red things wouldn't take them from him."

"Damn," Wade said.

"Why wouldn't they?" Tyler asked. "And why do they seem to not want anything to do with all you assholes?"

"It's a long walk," Richie said. "We'll fill you in."

***

They stood outside the wobbling portal, watching the fog shift away from the oncoming cavalry, which looked like a black mass in the distance.

Richie had noticed that the shapeless light had gotten smaller since he'd last gone through it, their window for escape shrinking by the second.

Shelly stood with two bloody stones cupped in one hand.

Together, they all waited as the black mass took shape, walking toward them, details forming. Hundreds of eyes, hundreds of teeth. A dozen Red Demons pulled bundles of dried intestines connected to a bony platform on fleshy wheels, the wet edges coated with the dust of the wasteland. The Skinless Ones stood atop the platform, huddled over a naked, emaciated man with half a recognizable face. Wisps of withered hair jutted out of his sunburned scalp. A grey beard lined the one good half of his face. The bad half was all red rot, lined with boils. The skin around his eye had receded, making the faded pupil eerily noticeable, and his lips were dried and cracked, forming a grin where it shouldn't have been.

As the convoy approached and the features of the prisoner became more apparent, the revenant of Helana let out a gasp.

"Dad?" she whispered.

She walked forward, wasting no time.

With his palms resting against the handle of his sword, propped up in the dirt by the blade, Wade said, "So she really died on purpose so that she could go to the underworld, inhabit a dead body, and try to find her dead dad, who was put here by her own mom, so that he could fix the portal-thingy after that Jackson dude blew it up?"

When no one answered, Wade gave an amused whistle. "Hell of a Saturday night."

Richie followed Helena and watched as the convoy stopped. The sea of Red Demons parted as Helena made her way to the platform.

Before they got to it, one of the Skinless Ones kicked Helena's father. A light tap was all it took to send him hurtling to the ground in a cloud of ash and dust. The man must have weighed around a hundred thirty pounds.

"Hey!" Helena said.

The Skinless Ones laughed.

It was a not-so-subtle reminder of who they'd allied themselves with.

Savages.

Helena cupped her father's head in her hands while Richie waited on standby, knowing he'd need to help lift the man up soon.

"Dad?" Helena said. "It's me. It's Helena. I know I don't look like it, but I'm really here."

He turned his head toward her, revealing the ruined side of his face.

"God, what did they do to you?" Helena asked.

"You are lucky," a Skinless One said from the platform.

"He is not fully transitioned," another said.

"Though he has developed ..." another said.

"A taste for despair," another said.

They all laughed.

"You're not my daughter," Helena's father said. The words came out slowly, painfully, as if restricted by a useless set of dried lungs, but it showed that he was alive and more conscious than his demon counterparts.

Helena spoke softly, and Richie knew the Helena inside of the body was crying for her father even though the corpse couldn't. "It's a long story," Helena said, "but it's me. We have so much to catch up on, but Dad ... we really need you right now."

35

"Everyone, my father, Ernest Vanderloo," Helena said to the group as she brought her half-rotted dad toward them.

Ernest looked worse than the Red Demons, since he still had some semblance of humanity, but a humanity that was getting devoured by a plague of bodily degradation. Still, as Ernest stood there half-decomposed next to his daughter, who inhabited a dead, scorched body, Richie sensed their longing for each other in the way they touched, the tenderness of their movements. It was a hopeful moment in two worlds of chaos: The one they were leaving and the one they were entering again.

"I don't imagine you all have any clothes?" Ernest asked.

Richie removed what was left of his shirt and wrapped it around the man's frail waist, figuring that even with the blood and soot soaked into the fabric, it was better than nothing.

"Wish we were meeting under better circumstances, Sir," Wade said.

Shelly reached out her arm, displaying the stones. "I hear you may know what to do with these."

Ernest took the stones—one in each hand—and held them close to his face. "It's been so long. When did I use these?" He looked at Shelly. "What year is this?"

"You've been here for a year, Dad," Helena said. "And we really need you to remember fast."

"What do you need me to do with these?" Ernest asked Helena.

"Do you remember building a gateway? One that led to this world?" Helena asked.

The man struggled, reaching back into the depths of his mind, connecting pieces of a puzzle as if his brain had been blended into puree.

Richie stepped forward and looked him in the eye. "Ernest. Hi. My name's Richie Stull. I have a child on the way. I have every intention of getting back to my family. So whatever dots you're trying to connect, do it now. Listen to me ... William Brenadeir. Does that name ring a bell?"

Ernest blinked rapidly. "Brenadeir ... Yes."

Richie continued, "He contracted you to make a portal that would give you infinite knowledge, yeah?"

"I ..." Ernest struggled.

What was the word Aiden had used? Remembering, Richie said, "Prosperity."

Ernest's eyes snapped to Richie's. "Prosperity ... Darlene."

"Yeah, Darlene, your wife," Richie said. "She's the one who put you here. She's on the other side of that glowing blob right there. She won't be expecting you to come through. If you could see her again, what would you do?"

Something clicked within Ernest—a sudden acuteness that he hadn't possessed before. "I'd drag her into this dimension and have her face the horrors I have. I'd want her pain to last for an eternity while the beasts of this world suck the life from her body until she's bone dry."

Holy shit, that got real dark real fast, Richie thought.

Shelly said, "You have a chance to make sure your wife and everyone else like her never feeds anyone to this place ever again."

"How?" Ernest asked.

"We're going to feed Darlene and her friends to it instead," Shelly answered. "Then, with your help, we're going to close that gate."

A Skinless One jumped off the platform. Its ankle snapped, and the hive mind sighed with pleasure.

It walked slowly toward Richie and Shelly as the Red Demons stood, waiting. "You two ..." It gagged and cuffed its mouth, then removed its hand. "Time is of the essence. If the veil fades, whoever is on the other side will be stuck. I am going through. Should I be stuck,

I will feast on your world for as long as there's anything to feast upon. You understand this?"

"We all go. All at once," Richie said. "You control these things, right? Let 'em loose."

"On your command," the Skinless One said.

Richie, Shelly, Helena, and Ernest turned and walked toward the shimmer.

"Is he up for this?" Shelly asked Helena.

"Yes," Helena said. "He'll do it. I know he will."

"We doin' this now?" Wade asked.

Richie nodded, and Wade raised his broadsword, turning toward the floating spiral.

Tyler climbed to his feet, grunting through the pain as blood seeped out of his calves and forearms.

With a demon army at their back, the contestants stood, ready for their final round, stained with blood, covered in dirt. Richie was running off of pure adrenaline circulating through his body quickly enough that he didn't question the hunger in his belly, the dryness in his mouth, the time of night, and how desperately he wanted his cheek to touch a pillow.

Helena put a hand on her father's shoulder. "Dad, I've always been proud of you. I need you to make me proud one last time. Even when you can't see me, I'll be with you. From now on, I'll always be with you."

"You can't come with us, can you?" Shelly asked.

"Something tells me I can do more from this side," Helena answered. "It's a miracle this body's lasted as long as it has. I'll be in your ear, though."

Miracle. Richie chuckled somberly. What had he witnessed over the past few hours if not a series of miracles? Miracles were what the Skinless Ones offered and what the People of the Red Night extracted. Impossible feats, wondrous sights, all available to the highest bidder.

"Helena," Ernest said, "there's so much I want to—"

"We'll talk soon, Dad," Helena said. "I promise. I got you now. And I am *so* going to haunt the shit out of you." She laughed, then addressed the group. "I'm haunting the shit out of *all* of you."

Richie grinned.

"You see my mom," Helena said. "Bring her here."

"With pleasure," Wade said.

Richie looked back at the Skinless Ones. "Send them in."

The Skinless Ones laughed. The one with the bum ankle stepped in line with the contestants, then said, "Bring us their despair. Go."

The demon horde rushed forward, rustling past the contestants and leaping through the portal.

Richie held the battle axe across his chest. "Everyone ready?"

"Fuck yeah," Wade said.

"Fuck yeah," Shelly repeated.

"Yep," Tyler said.

"Yes," Ernest said.

A Red Demon appeared through the portal, pulling something quick through the light with it. A man in a white hazmat suit, kicking and screaming, materialized as he was dragged into the hell dimension.

"So it begins," the Skinless One said.

Richie took the first step.

Inmates run the asylum, he thought.

36

In a flash of white light, Richie was back in the arena with the metal grating against his feet. The metal frame, twisted and bent, hung over his head. The demon army ran with no uniformity, zigzagging, stumbling into each other, leaping off the metal platform, climbing into the stands. Soon, they'd be like ants pouring into a tunnel network.

"Seal the arena!" a voice shouted from the overhead speakers. "Contain the intruders!"

Panicked screams drew Richie's attention toward the control panel, where Brenadeir's grunts were swarmed by Red Demons slashing into their hazmat suits. They'd been working to reassemble the wiring and fix the dashboard, Richie figured, but they hadn't been able to fix it without the missing stones.

"Wade and Tyler," Richie commanded, "make sure no one gets to Ernest while he's fixing the gate."

"Hell no. I'm coming with you," Wade said.

"I'll watch his back," Tyler said, limping behind Ernest as he hobbled through a crowd of Red Demons, making his way to the control panel with a handful of bloody stones.

"We will protect them," the Skinless One said.

"Then they'll be sitting ducks," Wade said. "What are we gonna do when the snipers come out?" He pointed toward the rafters.

Richie turned to the Skinless One. "Can you get your people up to those rafters?

The Skinless One laughed, then raised its hands. "Climb."

And they did, scattering like cockroaches, leaping down from the metal platform and toward the stands. They crawled over each other, forming a ladder with their bodies, quickly ascending.

"Look alive," Shelly said, nudging Richie's arm with her axe handle. "Let's go find Brenadeir."

Machine gun fire cracked. Brandier's soldiers took their places up high and opened fire on the mass crawling up the sides of the underground stadium.

Richie and Shelly sprinted and bounded off the metal platform in as shell casings rattled above them. Wade seethed as he sped up his damaged legs to follow them, then screamed from the impact when his feet hit the ground.

Richie glanced back and saw the Skinless One taking its time to walk across the platform.

Some help he'd be.

They came to the large double doors that led to the waiting room. Richie pulled on the handles.

The doors didn't budge.

"Shit," Richie said.

Wade threw a hard swing of his sword at the door, only to have the blade rattle off.

"What do we do without a way in?" Shelly asked.

Richie looked up at the swarm forming upward lines, rising one body on top of the other. Even as the soldiers fired, even as they picked off an unlucky demon, more would rise up. More Red Demons came through the portal, filling in the mass like a wave slashing in slow motion against a sea wall. They spilled over the platforms as the soldiers retreated, shooting, panicking, helpless.

"What's that, about three stories up?" Richie asked.

Wade grunted. "Might as fuckin' well."

They ran to one cluster. Shelly went first, then Wade, then Richie. Their hands struggled for purchase, gripping the skin of the Red Demons while still clutching their weapons.

Until a sea of arms guided their bodies upward, the horde assisting them in their ascent.

As Shelly made it to the top, the Skinless One yelled, "The enemy of my enemy!"

She fell over the railing and onto the platform. Wade followed, then Richie.

As soon as Richie touched down on the platform, a marksman flew off of it in the other direction. Travelling downward on the whims of gravity, the goon's tailbone landed with a thud on the side of the metal platform, and his body jackknifed in the wrong direction.

Richie picked himself up, brushing shell casings against the flooring, and together they moved toward the carnage, past other screaming bodies being passed around as if on a conveyor belt.

The platform fed into a single room that was lined floor to ceiling with gun racks, but no guns. There must have been a dozen marksmen, Richie thought, but the looted room would suggest there'd once been three dozen rifles.

Static popped on the speaker system. "People of the Red Night! Protect the Great Redeemer at all costs! Do not let the intruders get to the Great Redeemer!"

"They took all the guns," Shelly said. She picked up one stray assault rifle off the floor and checked the magazine. "Everything here is empty."

"We're *literally* bringing knives to a gunfight?" Wade asked.

"You don't have to go," Richie said. "But if we don't get our hands on that book, we're dead anyway. So many people will die slow, painful deaths, if they're even allowed to die at all. I'll take my chances."

Richie marched toward the elevator at the end of the room, battle axe at the ready. He pressed the button to call it up and waited, eager to step in and let the doors close him off from the carnage, if only for a moment.

"It was just a joke," Wade said, stepping up shoulder-to-shoulder with Richie. "You know, bring a knife to a gun f—"

"I know, Wade," Rich said.

Wade tilted his neck, cracking it. "Let's do this."

They waited.

A gaggle of Red Demons surrounded them, panting, wheezing.

"What the hell are we gonna tell people?" Wade asked. "You know ... *if* we make it out of this?"

"I don't think we've gotten that far in the plan yet," Shelly answered.

"I'm gonna tell my girlfriend that she was right to be skeptical," Richie said.

Wade chuckled. "I'm sorry for being such a dick. I know I fuckin' suck. When this is all over, first round's on me."

"Deal," Richie replied.

"Second and third too," Shelly added.

The elevator door slid open, and they all stepped in, followed by the footsteps of Red Demons—their own little monster battalion, bobbing excitedly.

Richie hit the "4" on the control panel.

The door slid closed, muffling the chaos.

Again they waited. Richie's mind spiraled in anticipation for what he'd see on the other side of that elevator when the door opened.

The elevator dinged, and he got his answer.

The door slid open, revealing a man in his sixties with slicked-back grey hair and a tightly trimmed beard aiming the barrel of a handgun at Richie's eye level. Even with the gun partially obscuring the man's face, Richie recognized him as Mr. Melroy, the man who had given the contestants a tour earlier that night, long before they knew what they were in for.

Melroy's finger squeezed.

37

Richie ducked as a bullet flew past his skull, the gunshot deafening. When he looked up, a flash of metal pierced through Mr. Melroy's jaw, forming a line to the top of his head, catching grey hair on the way out.

Wade held the broadsword steady under the man's jaw and yelled, "Grab the gun!"

Shelly dropped her axe and ripped the handgun from the man's limp hand.

The Red Demons leapt out claws-first—excited, eager.

Richie looked past Mr. Melroy, who'd just been stabbed clean through the brain. It was the same corridor he'd seen before, with the ugly purple carpet and the green doors. Only this time, there were men in suits and women in dresses filing out through the doors with guns in their hands.

"Shit," Richie said.

Shelly took a shooter's stance and shot over the dead man's shoulder.

POP! POP! POP!

The People of the Red Night fired back, ripping holes in the Red Demons and the human shield that was Mr. Melroy as Shelly, Richie, and Wade moved forward as a unit.

The Red Demons landed on their victims like lions hunting prey, ceasing the gunfire.

"It's up ahead!" Richie yelled. "On the other side of the stairwell!"

As soon as he said the word "stairwell", a head popped up from the bottom of the railing. The long barrel of a shotgun followed with it.

Aiden Prince.

A Red Demon pounced onto the banister, its eye cast downward toward Aiden.

Aiden sent a shotgun blast and fleshy, bony viscera skyward, giving the ceiling a fresh paint job, compliments of the Red Demon's head.

"Richie! What the hell are you thinking?!" Aiden yelled. "This is very, *very* disappointing!"

A door opened to Richie's left, and the glint of a rifle muzzle followed soon after

Richie swung his axe like a golf club, cutting through the hand of whoever was on the other side of the doorframe. He didn't care. Regardless of who was carrying it, they wanted carnage.

And he'd give them carnage.

A line of bullets cut through the ceiling as the muzzle tilted upward.

Richie charged into the room, axe first, settling the blade into the gunman's face. The back of the man's head fell onto a dusty bedpost, and the impact gave the axe a final bit of *umph*, separating the man's face into two halves.

Congressman John Stallings looked back at Richie, with one eye pointed toward one corner of the room, the other pointed at the opposite corner. Exposed by a split-open jaw, his throat pumped a gurgle of blood onto Richie's chin.

"Please don't kill me," a woman's voice said from Richie's side.

He turned to see Congresswoman Jennifer Parsons, hands raised and leaning against a dresser, with nowhere left to back into.

"I had no idea any of this would happen," she said.

While that was certainly true, Richie didn't have a moment to ask which parts of the night she didn't expect, though he could assume. Red Demons flooded in as she screamed "No!" and pulled her out of the room and toward the stairwell.

Toward Aiden.

"Richie!" Aiden yelled from outside the room.

Another shotgun blast.

The Red Demons squealed.

Another blast.

Wade yelped in pain.

And then, an agonizing high-pitched shriek rang through the corridor, up through the stairs, through the entirety of the mansion.

"You insufferable little thugs! I'll kill you all like dogs!" Aiden yelled.

Richie ripped the axe out of Congressman Stallings' face, then poked his head out of the room. Lumps of ruined demon bodies lined the carpet, with a pile consisting of Red Demons and Congresswoman Parsons' insides lying at the feet of Aiden Prince, a man so crazed he would gun down his own kind now to stop the demons.

Two Red Demons grabbed their heads, whining like buzzsaws. Aiden ripped holes through each of them.

Wade crawled away from Aiden, his hands mashing through Parsons' large intestine, his shattered, bloody leg trailing behind him.

On the opposite side of the corridor, Shelly hid behind an open door, shielding herself from Aiden. She held her gun up to Richie, showing that the slide was racked, that the gun had run dry.

"You pieces of shit have ruined so much!" Aiden yelled, cocking the shotgun. "I don't know how you did it, and I don't care. If I can't send you back to hell, I'll just settle for blowing you to bits instead."

"You rich fucks are all the same," Wade said, eyes watery, seething through the pain of his damaged leg. "Talking too damn much." Slowly, he crawled toward the dagger inches in front of him, the one he'd fastened into his belt before they'd gone back through the gate. He locked eyes with Richie and nodded.

From the floor below, gunfire replaced the shrieks.

"You hear that?" Aiden asked. "That's the sound of you all losing. That's the contingency, and *that's* what people like you lot do. You lose. What was your plan, huh?"

Richie poked his head out again. Wade was getting closer to the dagger.

"You wanna know?!" Richie yelled. "We were gonna take that Great Corruptor or Redeemer or whatever the fuck! Try to get to it before you all did!"

Aiden laughed. "Smart boy. I see I showed you too much."

Wade fingered the handle of the dagger.

"Yeah, that's kinda what you people do, right?" Richie said. "Show off your toys and think that people like us are too stupid to know what to do with them?"

"Remember what I told you last time we were in this very corridor?" Aiden asked. "I told you smarts would only get you so far. You can be smart and be a good follower. That's all you'll ever be, Richie. All of you. Bottom feeders."

"I'd rather be a bottom feeder than the dumbest asshole in the room right now," Richie said. "Can you guess who out of all of us, that is?"

Aiden took a moment to answer, maybe trying to repair his fragile ego. "Maybe this one on the ground here. The one I'm about to kill."

"Hey!" Richie yelled, getting Aiden's attention again.

Wade clutched the handle.

"I've been meaning to ask," Richie said. "How did you really lose that finger?"

Aiden laughed. "What, you mean this one?" He lowered his shotgun, removed his shooting hand from it, and raised his middle finger to Richie.

Wade flipped over and hurled the dagger at Aiden.

Richie sprinted as the dagger caught Aiden in the forearm. Aiden seethed and prepared to whip the shotgun around.

With two hands gripping the axe, Richie threw it forward.

Aiden dodged it, letting off a panic shot and ripping a hole in the wall. Spinning, he fell to the ground. He loaded another round. Aimed.

Shelly kicked the barrel, and the ceiling above them splintered.

Richie grabbed the gun and ripped it away.

Shelly pulled the dagger out of Aiden's forearm and stabbed his shoulder.

He screamed and swung his fist at the side of her head. Dazed, Shelly lopped onto her side.

Before Richie could aim the shotgun, Aiden grabbed it, and they struggled in a vicious tug of war, slamming into one wall, then the other.

"Up here!" Aiden yelled. "They're up here! Kill them!"

Wade grabbed Aiden's leg, but Aiden kicked it free and put his heel in Wade's nose. Then, Aiden slammed Richie against the wall again.

"They're unarmed!" Aiden yelled. He lowered his voice, bringing his face close to Richie's. "You underestimated me." He laughed. "You thought because I hadn't been in the games I couldn't hold my own in a fight. Feeling smart now, Richie?"

Every exhausted muscle in Richie's body tensed as he gripped the shotgun. Footsteps clattered up the stairs to his left.

A wave of bloodied suits, ripped button-down shirts, and gory dresses appeared at the top of the stairs.

"Shoot this son of a bitch!" Aiden said through gritted teeth.

"Move. I can't get a clear shot," someone in the crowd responded.

"Oh, fine." Aiden headbutted Richie, and a jolt of pain shot through Richie's skull.

Aiden pulled the gun away, rubbing his forehead as Richie fell. "Fuck!" He aimed the barrel down at the top of Richie's head. "Goddammit, Richie. Just because you've been such a tremendous pain in my ass, I'm considering keeping you alive, just so you can watch your sweet little Kate die slowly. After that, I'll make you watch us reestablish the games. And I'll make you watch the games. I'll make you watch everyone who loses go through that gate, and then, just when you realize how much you've lost, how much you've always been destined to lose, maybe then I'll consider ending your life for you. It'll be a mercy kill."

"Do it!" a voice shouted from the other side of the stairwell.

The mob parted, all heads turning toward the voice.

Darlene Vanderloo stood at the far end of the corridor, the Great Corruptor open in her hands, with the wrist Richie had sliced into bound in a cast.

"What the hell are you doing, Darlene? Finish it!" Aiden commanded.

"I've read enough," Darlene said. "They've taken plenty of our own to feed on. This is only a minor setback."

"They've turned on us," Aiden said. "You really think we can trust them now? The Skinless Ones might not be able to die, but their minions can. We take all of them away. Make the Skinless Ones desperate to regrow their community. This has always been the plan if things ever went sideways. And things are pretty fucking sideways, right now, Darlene!"

"William can broker a deal again," Darlene responded. "That's what he does. We can't afford to lose their power. Just kill these lowlifes and we'll figure everything out."

Shelly moaned. Wade was unconscious. A small battalion of angry elites was prepared to pounce on Richie. He could have sobbed. He wanted to. But he didn't want to give Aiden the satisfaction.

Then ...

Richie, I'm on the way.

That voice ...

Richie laughed.

"What's funny?" Aiden asked.

Richie continued to laugh.

Aiden looked over to the crowd. "Kid's finally lost it."

To Richie's right, the gears of the elevator whirred.

"Well, look at that," Aiden said. "Even more reinforcements. You see, Richie, true power is control. *We* control the Skinless Ones and their horde. *We* control—what the hell is so goddamn funny?!"

"Something you said," Richie replied. "About me underestimating you in a fight." He chuckled. "You've seen us go through hell. We're exhausted, spent, starved. We've literally been to hell and back—*hell*, dude. You basically jumped in the ring in the ninth round with weighted gloves and tagged in. And you expect me to acknowledge any kind of superiority?" Richie howled with laughter. "And just a couple hours ago, that woman ..." He pointed past the crowd to Darlene. "... tried to kill me just to spite you, but now you're working *with* her. All because you can't afford to ..." He raised his hands and made air quotes. "... lose power. God, you're pathetic."

"Changed my mind," Aiden said. "I *am* just gonna kill you here."

The elevator dinged.

"Well, look at that," Richie said as the elevator door opened. "Even more reinforcements."

Aiden glanced at what was in the elevator and yelled, "Darlene!"

38

The revenant of Helena ran out of the elevator, leading a wave of blackened, decaying bodies.

The crowd at the opposite end of the hall opened fire at the bodies—very *dead* bodies propelled by something other than life. The bullets did nothing but riddle them with divots.

Aiden turned. Aimed. *CLICK*. "Shit!" He dropped the shotgun and turned to run.

Richie grabbed him by the collar, stopping him, and looked him in the eye. "Feeling smart now?" He nudged Aiden into the rushing wave.

Richie pounced onto Wade, rolling him toward the opposite wall.

Helena wrapped herself around Shelly, forming a barrier before the rest of the undead army collided with them.

The crowd took Aiden and passed him backward in the most vicious display of crowd surfing. One limb came off, then another, until his torso hit the ground, becoming a wet, sloppy doormat for them to tread on.

The gunfire continued as the elites retreated backward, spraying skin and blood along the walls and ceiling.

Richie wanted to scream, "How?!"

Before he could, a hand lowered in front of his face, reaching out for him. Dried muscle tissue hung from an exposed bone in the forearm of a corpse, and pale, dead eyes stared into his. "Come on, Richie. Don't let me die in vain."

Perplexed, Richie gripped the hand and let the corpse pull him up. "Vince?!" he yelled over gunfire.

The corpse's cheek lifted, and white pus popped out from underneath the eye. It all connected for Richie: He was in the presence of a zombie army powered by the angry souls of those who died in the game.

"Get the book!" Helena shouted.

The corpse that Vince inhabited jolted, recoiling from the impact of a bullet in his back. He didn't wince or grunt or even so much as shrug. "Follow me," he said to Richie.

Vince sprang forward into the crowd, into the screams and cracks of gunfire, the blood spatter, the stray heads and limbs. He lowered his shoulder into the legs of a man in a tattered three-piece suit, sending the man's feet skyward.

Richie caught the man by the legs and slammed his head into the ground, bending his head sideways in a crunch that was muffled by the surrounding chaos.

Richie let out a primal scream.

In his field of vision, past the flailing limbs, past a woman in a sparkly dress having her nose bitten off, Darlene Vanderloo flipped through the pages in the Great Redeemer, finding her place.

Vince picked up an M16 off the blood-stained carpet and tossed it into Richie's hands.

Before Richie opened fire, he watched as Vince leapt over the railing on the stairwell, falling into the cult members attempting to flee and knocking them over like bowling pins.

A bullet spiked through Richie's shoulder. The adrenaline absorbed the pain. Richie pulled the trigger, shooting at any head that remained in the corridor, anyone who stood between him and Darlene.

When the magazine ran dry, he swung the M16 like an axe, cracking the last cluster of skulls in his way until he had a clear beeline at Darlene.

Darlene found her page.

Richie rounded the stairwell.

Darlene drew breath.

Richie sprinted, closing the distance between them.

39

T he book fell to the ground.

Darlene gasped as a bony hand squeezed against her throat. Richie stopped.

Ernest Vanderloo appeared behind his wife, speaking into her ear. "Remember, dear," he said, "I helped design this place. I know all of its tricks."

Panting, Richie turned to present the fallen book to whomever was left of the People of the Red Night, to show them that they had lost, but all that was left was bits of flesh and torn bodies, with the undead corpses that had ripped through them quickly filing down the stairs to cut through whomever remained breathing.

A couple of sounds squeaked out of Darlene's mouth, and Richie knew she was attempting to say, "Ernest?"

Helena walked forward, her raw feet mashing through piles of human sludge. "Hello, Mom. I found Dad. It doesn't look like he's all that happy to see you, though."

Ernest threw Darlene to the ground.

Coughing, Darlene reached for the book with her casted hand.

Richie stepped on her wrist, and she yelped.

He looked at Ernest, then Helena. "Sorry."

Helena shrugged.

"Ernest?" Darlene said, crawling backward. "My god, how did you ... What's happened to you?" She turned to Helena. "And who the fuck are you?"

"Where's Brenadeir?" Richie asked while bending down to grab the book.

"Long gone from here," Darlene said. "You think he'd risk his life for this?"

"The place is on lockdown," Richie replied.

"An escape route," Ernest said. "He wanted this place designed to keep everyone inside but him. Because everyone is expendable. Even my dear Darlene."

"It's not too late," Darlene said. "We can reform the People of the Red Night. Richie, you hate me, I know you do. People like you hate all of us because you can never *be* like us. Never have what we have. But you need me. I'm connected. I can invite all of the filthy rich people you despise here, and you can watch them all get carried away to hell."

"Mom ..." Helena said, "stop groveling."

"Why do you keep calling me that?" Darlene asked.

"I always knew she was a special girl," Ernest said. "And you went and sentenced her to death."

"And in doing so, you set the wheels in motion," Helena said. "You destroyed this empire the minute you put me in the Night Games."

"Fuckin' rich people," Richie said.

"Fuckin' rich people," Shelly repeated, joining the group. "And you're wrong. About two things, actually. One: We don't need you. We formed an alliance with those monsters, which means ... we basically know everything now. We can find Brenadeir easily. Second: It's not that we don't like you because you're rich; we don't like you because you're an asshole."

"So, what, then?" Darlene said. "You all just kill me and walk away? It doesn't matter what pact you made with the Skinless Ones, Brenadeir will come for you. He has resources you can't imagine, in places you would think impossible. You'll never be safe—"

"I think that's enough, dear," Ernest said, kneeling down to her. "It's time for you to go."

"Go where?"

"We're not going to kill you. You're about to go through days, months, years of constant torture. You'll be helpless as you succumb to the changes in your body structure, the starvation that becomes an empty void, until you realize that, while yes, you still yearn for food, there's something else that you desire. Something so sweet, so euphoric, it's unlike anything you've ever tasted."

"What the hell are you saying, Ernest?"

"I can smell you, dear."

"They're gonna love you down there," Richie said.

40

As the last body trailed off kicking and screaming through the portal, Richie knew that soon the screams would be silenced and transformed to vomit. He felt no remorse. Those who surrounded him, who fought with him—Shelly, Wade, Tyler, Ernest, and the two corpses who were Vince and Helena—looked onward with that same tired, glazed-over stare.

Before the lone Skinless One departed, Richie requested the infinite knowledge its people had promised. He asked for the whereabouts of one man. The one who fled before seeing his kingdom crumble. The Skinless One placed a palm on Richie's head.

And suddenly, Richie knew.

While the screams no longer reverberated through the halls of Brenadeir's mansion, they still echoed in Richie's eardrums like a perpetual aftershock, but it didn't stop him from enjoying that drink with his new friends. Brenadeir's alcohol collection was among the finest, after all.

As they drank, Helena described her newfound ability as what she called a spirit broker. Her spinal column collapsed, and she asked to be taken back through the portal so she could dump the body. Less clean up.

She had a major role to play in what came next, and she was very excited about her next host.

Richie couldn't take too much time to decompress. The sun would soon be up and Kate would be pissed, worried, and on a mission to find her missing man. But she couldn't know about this place or the crazy, otherworldly shitshow he endured. Not yet. Not until he knew exactly what to say. He had to change out of his thrifted outfit tainted with sweat, blood, and dark bile. It didn't take him long to find a guest room with an overnight bag containing some sweatpants and a plain black t-shirt. The dead bastard whom these clothes belonged to wouldn't be needing them.

———

Richie took his own car home.

The sun was just beginning to rise as he tiptoed into his apartment, careful to not wake Kate. Staying quiet was an awful task with cut, swollen, heavy feet. He'd done a decent job at scrubbing the matted blood off his face in a Brenadeir estate sink, but his chest swelled at the anticipation of taking the most goddamn satisfying shower of his life. The shock of the night's events had his lips sealed shut, jaw clenched, and he wasn't in the state of mind to offer up so much as a white lie.

He watched the blacks and reds slide from his body, down his legs, and pool at the bottom of the shower, then eventually swirl and disappear down the drain. Richie stood underneath the showerhead, cocooned in the ambiance of water hitting acrylic. Soon, the hot water no longer burned his scars.

Finally, there was something other than the echoes of violence to fill his ears, to drown out the screams—

"What the hell happened to you?"

Richie jolted, gasping. Kate stood under the frame of the bathroom door in an oversized tee shirt, hair messy in that way Richie loved. She eyed his naked body—the bruises, the scrapes. Her mind was running wild, attempting to draw some line between a simple networking event and his current physical condition.

"Oh my god," she said in a quieter, breathy tone, overcome with worry. "What ... the hell ... happened to you?"

Richie turned the shower dial, cutting off the water. He had the entire ride back to think about what he might say to Kate, but his brain was fried and threatening to shut down.

He took a deep breath. "It's so good to see you. You have *no idea* how good it is to see you."

"Did you … get mugged?" Kate asked.

"Some things happened tonight. Some … really weird things. But I want you to know that you and me … We're gonna be okay."

"Richie, you look like you should be in a hospital. What the fuck are you talking about? Who did this to you?"

"I'm saying that I don't have to work construction anymore. You and I will never have to work again."

"You're freakin' me out, babe—"

"There's something I have to do," Richie said. "I'm heading out tomorrow morning. I need you to not ask any questions, please. Just know that I love you very much, and we're going to be—"

"Who are you?" Kate gently put her palms to his cheeks. "Because the Richie Stull I know doesn't keep secrets from me."

"It's not that simple."

"When has it ever been? We are in this together. The three of us." Kate patted her stomach. "So I'm gonna take a look at your scars, and you're going to tell me everything. Got it?"

Richie sighed, then slowly lowered himself into the tub with a groan. "You're really not gonna believe this."

Epilogue

Above the iron gate, the sun was beginning to set.

Angus Goodman, a man with salt and pepper stubble and generously-placed hair plugs, stared up through the cursive "B" that hung across the vertical bars.

He hadn't driven in months—he had a driver for that—but William Brenadeir would only allow guests to come alone. No drivers, no chauffeurs, no escorts or mistresses. They could use no GPS navigation to get there, and if they did, they'd be detected.

Total secrecy. Complete anonymity.

It was all the better for Angus. Whatever secrets they were keeping, he knew they had to be good. He was new to the world of elites thanks to a massive sale on a tech startup he built, or rather, built up the valuation of. The technology was shit, the underlying code archaic, and by the time the acquiring company found out, he'd have dumped the stock and would have too much money tied up in assets to be bothered with a single fuck. But, though he was green to this *Eyes-Wide-Shut*-style secret cabal type shit, he knew that all the red tape surrounding this event made it too good to pass up.

The gates to the Brenadeir Estate opened.

The pavement, fountain, the myriad of windows and balconies, the million-dollar vehicles parked outside, it all made the young wannabe-hotshot in Angus squeal.

A woman with dark hair in a suit greeted him at the front door, her hands behind her back. "Angus Goodman, welcome to Brenadeir Estate," she said.

Taken aback, Angus said, "You know of me?"

"As a staff member, it's my responsibility to know all of the guests and ensure they are comfortable once inside." She grinned cordially.

Angus was flattered—feeling a little lucky, even—and, for that reason, the next thing he said was, "Pity. You know me, but I don't know you. What's your name?"

"Raven," the woman said.

Angus flashed his most charming smile. "Will I see you inside, Raven?"

She returned the smile, though there was something off-putting about it. Something he couldn't put his finger on. "I'm sure you will," she answered. "Welcome to the Red Night. Please be prepared to surrender your phone and any other electronic devices once inside."

Phoneless and with only his wits to guide him, Angus floated from millionaire to millionaire around the banquet hall, rubbing elbows with CEOs and portfolio managers and politicians and oligarchs, many of whom he recognized. He hoped the smile wasn't giving him away—that childish grin he might've worn as a teenager recognizing a pornstar in public.

All of these people were members of this exclusive Red Night cult, something that would presumably make them, and, more important-ly, Angus Goodman, incredibly wealthy.

He'd made it to the top of the social hierarchy and wondered if he'd hit the ceiling. Wondered if he could be content with his earnings, maybe live off of interest and dividends for the rest of his life wooing models with fancy things. But the people at this event seemed to believe there was no ceiling, that William Brenadeir wasn't just some titan of finance, but some kind of wizard—A *god* even.

And then, his entrance ...

Hot damn, William Brenadeir's entrance.

He stood above them in a loft—indeed, like a god—eye-level with a sparkling chandelier.

The crowd beamed, sighed, and raised their glasses to the white-haired man in a grey three-piece suit as he rested his hands on the wooden railing, his veneers blindingly white.

"Allow me to introduce myself. I am William Lee Brenadeir. Many of you may have heard whispers of what we do on nights such as these. If you *have*, well ... someone has broken a very lengthy NDA."

Everyone belly laughed except Angus, but he recovered quickly. Apparently, NDAs were hilarious to this crowd.

"If you have caught wind of the so-called 'Night Games', I assure you, tonight will be slightly different. But, of course, it always starts with a total lockdown to ensure privacy."

Gears groaned as metal obstructions climbed down the doors and windows.

"Don't worry," Brenadeir continued. "They're set to reopen in three hours via an automatic timer. I couldn't get them open even if I wanted to. The automation is by design—again, for the purposes of privacy."

Angus' heart leapt. He hadn't expected this. Hadn't known that he'd be stuck in this for three hours. It wasn't too long. He could survive in a place as gorgeous as this.

"Soon, our representatives will be taking you in groups to our ... let's call it an underground lair."

The crowd chuckled.

Said representatives walked into view, flanking Benadier. Three men in their twenties to one side, a woman in her twenties and a man in his fifties on the other side, all dressed in black suits. The fifty-something-year-old man appeared to have an unsettling skin condition on one half of his face. His skin was discolored on one side, and his eye was pale.

"Now, I know you're all eager to see what gifts await you," Brenadeir said. "I surely can't wait for you to find out. Cheers."

Brenadeir had no glass to raise, and so he bowed instead.

The crowd drank to that, cheering as Brenadeir walked out of view, and only the staff members stared back at them. Not soon after, they turned away and disappeared as well.

Eager, Brenadeir had said.

Angus Goodman was very eager.

He was very eager, indeed.

———

Helena piloted William Lee Brenadeir's body back toward the leather sofa in the loft. She took a seat, letting Brenadeir's dead flesh sink into the cushions. The longer he was dead, the harder it was to keep him moving, if only because the meat was threatening to slide clean off of his bones.

"Good work, honey," her father said. "Now, what do you say we get you out of this body?"

Richie, Wade, Tyler, and Shelly joined them, filling in the circle.

"Everyone ready?" Richie asked the group.

They all nodded.

Richie nodded back. "Let the Night Games begin."

Acknowledgements

I would like to acknowledge my mother for carrying me in a crowded womb. Of course, I have to acknowledge my brother, Joey. He's always been a model of strength and perseverance both in creativity and in life. He's my hero, despite being a minute younger than me ... smh.

—Josh

Hey, Reader. If you've made to this page, you're the first I'd like to thank. I'll also tell you that when Josh and I set out to write this, we decided to keep each other in the dark about what we were planning for our halves. We had a general premise, and I had an idea of where I wanted it to end up. Josh handed me 100+ pages filled with distinct characters, a seedy world of haves and have-nots, and many, many dangling threads. Deciding how the story ended was one coolest, most exciting writing experiences I'd had.

So thanks, Josh, for giving me these amazing characters to play with when you had no idea how their stories would end. I was happy to send your characters to hell.

Of course, we have to thank some amazingly authors for lending their time and eyeballs to an early version of this book and giving it their blessings (Cursings?) in the form of a blurb. Theses heroes, in no particular order, are: Wendy Dalrymple, Isaac Nightingale, Damien Casey, A.D Jones, A.D. Aro, and Julie Hiner.

Big ups to our editor Nico Bell for taking this hodgepodge mashup between two writers and making it more coherent than the two of us ever could on our own.

And last but not least, special thanks to Mike Gianakos for gifting us with a kickass cover illustration and bringing this idea to life.

—Joey